"Power does not corrupt.
Fear corrupts…perhaps the fear
of the loss of power."

John Steinbeck

PREFACE

This is a story of corruption in the Georgia prison system. Our corrections officers should be held to a high standard, but this story shows that they are not. And why not? Because many supervisors are corrupt. Telling this story may put a shadow over our state's handling of the system, but it's a story that should and must be told. To understand how rampant the corruption is, and how dangerous—dangerous to good officers and to inmates who become confidential informants—this story starts at the beginning of my time as a corrections officer in the Georgia prison system. But first, just what is the "prison system" of Georgia? Just what is the Georgia Department of Corrections?

The GDC is the authority that oversees the thirty-five institutions that house between 40,000 to 50,000 convicted felons. The department has legal responsibility for about another 200,000 people who may be on state probation, parole, or other criminal connection ordered by the state courts.

To properly police and maintain constant control and supervision of those 40,000 to 50,000 incarcerated persons, the department must employ the largest internal police force in the state. That's close to 10,000 academy-trained and certified peace officers. There is a standard for this training called P.O.S.T., which stands for peace officers standards and training. This is the governing body of all law enforcement for training and conduct.

The large number of people just in uniform who work in the many state institutions create some very serious employment problems, problems the state has yet to master. A few of the most glaring problems for potential officers are low pay scale, substandard hiring practices, improper vetting of new hires, high expense of proper officer training, and the high cost of the latest technical equipment. It seems the most outstanding issue for potential hires is the working environment, and there is little that can be done to effect meaningful change.

In the system there seems to be a problem of corrupt officers. How is this possible? Well, inmates are wily. They work a system known as Downing the Duck. Here's how it works: an inmate closely observes an officer for a period of time, time which the inmate has in abundance. He observes how the officer dresses, how and when he laughs, how he relates to fellow employees, and how he perceives his job by the comments he makes about his work and family. The inmate then makes innocuous comments to the officer based on the information he has gleaned from his observations. The comments could be about anything: cars, sports, movies. Once the officer falls for the trap, the relationship has reached a new level, and conversations between the two become more frequent and more relaxed.

Between three percent and five percent of officers will become suckered into the Downing the Duck scheme and join the ranks of the corrupt. One of the problems these officers have is the inevitable attempt by the corrupting inmate to advance their relationship even further. That's when the critical career-altering decision occurs of either giving it all up to their supervisors, or giving in and getting more deeply involved with the inmate.

Officers get caught up in the cycle of increased demands of the corrupting inmates. In the beginning, the demands are for simple things like food or special treatment, then demands escalate for contraband items to be brought into the prison.

Fortunately, approximately ninety-seven percent of officers are not involved in corruption, except to try to eradicate it. The majority of officers are a credit to their very difficult, extremely dangerous, and demanding profession. Hopefully, after you read this story, you will take a minute to offer a prayer for them in thanksgiving for doing a good job for little reward and less acknowledgment.

You'll read about the great amount of tension that exists between officers and inmates and how this tension has a direct and significant effect on the daily interactions of both groups. The constant presence of stress on both officers and inmates can be blamed for the violent and near-violent incidents that take place every day. Imagine carrying a highly explosive device in your pocket and not knowing when it will go off; that's what it's like living with the ever-present tension in the prison system. And you'll see that for officers, there is tension outside of the prison system as well.

PROLOGUE

It was the noise. My eyes popped open. My wife jumped out of bed and I flew across and pushed her to the floor.

"Jeff!"

"Shh." I crab-walked to the window. The squeal of tires as a car shot down the street was all I could get. That and tail lights.

"Jeff?" My wife squeaked my name.

I blew out a breath. "Sorry, honey." I helped her off the floor. "Gunshots. Wait here." I grabbed my pants, slid into loafers, reached on the shelf for my service revolver, ran downstairs, and bolted out the front door.

My neighbor across the street peeked out his front door. When he saw me, he came out.

"Cripes, Jeff, what the hell was that?"

"You okay, Ben?" I stood and stared at his house. His front windows were shot out, his front door pockmarked. "Everybody OK in there?" I know I sounded panicked. My neighbor has a wife and three kids.

Ben was shaking. "Fine," he whispered. "No one's home. They're all at Katie's sister's." He took a deep breath and let it out from puffed cheeks. "What the hell just happened?"

What-the-hell-just happened is that those gunshots were meant for me.

CHAPTER ONE

It all started for me, Jeffrey Wiles, in August of 2002. I was fifty-five when my company downsized and I found myself out of a job. OK. So what to do now? I had a sit-down with my wife and with her blessing I embarked on an exciting new career. I joined the Georgia Department of Corrections, but had no idea just how exciting this new career would be. Exciting? How about dangerous? Before excitement and danger though, I had to go through the mundane.

I arrived at the Department of Corrections academy and training facility in Forsyth, Georgia, on a sultry August Monday morning. I was one of 167 new cadets. We would live and train at the center Monday through Friday for the next four weeks.

My initial thoughts that first morning were that my fellow cadets acted like teens away from their parents for the first time. Granted they may have been excited but they were jumping around and speaking at decibels as high as a hot rodder's radio.

Did I say teens? Oh yeah. I heard them talking about a basketball rivalry between two local high schools. But of course I was fifty-five, so anybody younger than thirty looked and acted like a teen to me. As I listened to the loud, immature foolishness going on among my fellow cadets, I asked myself if I belonged here.

Another thing—I had to have a physical before I was accepted, but there were lots of overweight cadets—some were so obese they had difficulty fitting into the wooden seats in the center's auditorium. How did they pass the physical? I found myself leaning toward my cynical side. Uh-oh.

Let me explain about trainees before I go any further. All of us had been cadets in various prisons throughout the system. Cadets are sort of like interns. We do what we're told, but like interns, we don't operate. We don't get involved with inmates; that involvement is done only by trained and certified state peace officers with the powers of arrest.

Outfitted in white shirts and black pants, cadets watch and learn and do routine jobs like clerical filing and errand running. Most cadets "intern" from one to four weeks until a class at the academy opens up. In my case, I was at Rock Quarry State Prison for just three days. I learned very little of prison life. Not good.

We were assigned roommates the first thing. I thought I had lucked out with my roommate. Willie Sanders was twenty-five, and a nice guy who interned at Dodge State Prison. This was his first shot at a career. We teamed up quickly and sat through welcoming speeches from the head of the academy and instructors of the training classes. But I said I thought I had lucked out, not that I did luck out. Willie had a little problem, which I wouldn't discover until later that night.

After dozing through some of the speeches, we took a test called Peace Officers Standards and Training (P.O.S.T) that we had to pass to stay longer than this first day. I hate to take tests—never my strong suit—but this one was easy and almost all passed. Those who failed were dismissed. Their careers as new cadets were over.

The dorm room reminded me of an old Holiday Inn on the schedule for demolition. But the rooms looked clean and neat and included two single beds, one beat-up nightstand, and a 1960s-era push-button telephone. A large mirror was opposite the beds above two small wooden desks and hard chairs. Classy joint.

When we closed the door behind us, the first thing Willie said in his south Georgia country accent was, "There ain't no TV, they must be serious about us studyin' the dang class work." I learned fast that Willie Sanders was a religious man and did not use curse words. Dang was strong for him.

We were issued combination locks. Every morning we loaded our gear into our wardrobes and locked up. Strange, right? A bunch of cops and we have to lock up our stuff. We learned why. Every morning inmates came in to clean up and make the beds.

Every meal was in the large open cafeteria. There would be a few exceptions later on. Mealtime was an opportunity to meet fellow cadets from prisons across

Georgia. We all had opinions of what would be coming our way the next four weeks.

The food was edible, sort of like southern cafeterias I had frequented over the years. Most were unremarkable. The thing that made this cafeteria different and that bothered me the entire four weeks I was there was that all the meals were prepared by inmates. I wondered if they were in prison for poisoning people. Just as I wondered if our "maids" straightening our rooms had been arrested for burglary.

That first night Willie and I were bushed when we went to bed. But you know how it is in new surroundings and strange and uncomfortable beds. We didn't drift right off to sleep, so we talked well past the 11:00 p.m. lights-out. Drift off to sleep—hah! I discovered Willie's problem.

Willie Sanders snores and loud, very loud. Both of us had finally fallen off to sleep when I was awakened by a thunderous noise. A train? A steam engine? I hid under my pillow, stuffed toilet tissue in my ears, contemplated putting the pillow firmly over 300-pound Willie's face (bad idea).

I woke him up. Or tried to. First, I tapped on his shoulder—several times. No good. I slapped his face—gently. Finally, Willie came to. He sat up, swung his legs over the side of the bed and looked at me with a sheepish expression. The big guy was embarrassed and kept saying how sorry he was.

It seems even his loving wife makes him sleep downstairs at least a couple of times a week so she can get some much-needed sleep. I'm not as loving as his wife. It's going to be a long four weeks.

The alarm went off at 5 a.m. After breakfast we went to the yard for formation, inspection and roll call. The department's trainers acted like drill sergeants. They barked orders and ridiculed anyone they found lacking. They had no problem singling out particular trainees then proceeding to make fools of them.

On most days we would spend the day in classes and cover subjects that concerned managing inmates in a prison setting. Remember, we had done practically nothing prison-related as cadets in our respective prisons, so all of this stuff was new to us. The department made certain that every cadet was taught how prisons operated from the initial intake and classification of inmates to health care, housing, clothing, feeding, and discipline, both mild and severe.
We all probably had favorite—or at least preferred—classes. I liked those dealing with physical fitness, defensive tactics, offensive tactics, inmate control, and weapons qualification. As it turned out, those classes came in very handy during my career.

It was during the training class for weapons use and safety that it became way too obvious we really needed shooting practice. Either that, or some people should not handle guns. One of those people was in my class.

During a simple live-fire exercise on the outdoor range, a trainee who was not following simple instructions nearly killed another trainee on the lane next to his. This guy aimed his fully loaded and cocked weapon at the person just a few feet away. Everyone watched in absolute shock. The instructor reacted quickly and prevented what could have been a horrible incident. Oh, there's more. Another day on the firing range my target had ten rounds, but I fired only eight rounds. The extra two landed on the very edge of the paper target. The guy next to me had only six rounds on his target—very scattered rounds, so scattered that two landed on my target. All of us hoped the adage "practice makes perfect" would eventually apply here.

We had down time in the evening. Each night after dinner Willie and I would head over to the main building and its entertainment center. The dated TV had no cable so not many were watching it. Even more dated were the crippled pool tables and warped cues. To give you an idea of how boring the evening hours were, guys were actually shooting pool with the deformed cues and checking out the few channels on the cast-off TV. Another group of trainees sat on a threadbare puke green couch and matching dingy chairs with stuffing seeping through the seams. The décor here was as classy as the dorm rooms. And this group didn't seem very classy either. They were talking trash as if they were hanging out at a seedy bar with a few six-packs under their belts. Willie and I looked at each, grimaced, shrugged our shoulders, and left the party.

We took the outside cement walkway toward our building, and as we neared our dorm we could hear what sounded like a raucous party coming from our building. The closer we got, the louder the noise. Obviously we weren't the only ones hearing the racket, because several instructors bolted through the door and up the steps. One minute later, everything went quiet and lights were lowered. Are these guys and gals freshmen in college? What is this?

The next day at breakfast we all got the lowdown about the party from the resident gossips. The story is that four female cadets used their two rooms to party with at least six local high school guys that one of the girls met at the local Wal-Mart. The cadets admitted to being stoned on grass and drunk on beer. You guessed it. They were kicked out and sent back to their respective institutions to be dealt with by their wardens.

Four weeks passed quickly, and we all promised to stay in touch. I would miss big Willie's friendship, but not his thunderous snoring.

As newly sworn Georgia correctional peace officers sporting badges and the new rank insignia of CO1 pinned on our uniforms, we headed back home as new graduates ready to tackle the next phase of our careers. We were ready to put to use all that we had learned in our four short weeks of classes and the practical physical application of weapons and self-defense tactics.

CHAPTER TWO

Back home I reported to Rock Quarry State Prison. I'll admit I was excited and nervous to take on this new challenge and this completely new direction in my life.

First shift was assigned; I'm a morning person, so I was glad. I'd report at 5:45 and finish at 2 p.m. Or I thought I'd finish at 2. Those were the official hours for first shift but relief had to show up on time before anyone could leave his post. And "on time" didn't happen often.

The day began with a briefing 15 minutes before the start of the shift. Supervisors inspected uniforms, took attendance, reported on the previous shift, passed on department information, answered questions, and posted assignments for the day.

Rock Quarry State Prison (RQSP) is a close-security facility, which means it holds society's most dangerous convicted felons. From the outside most prisons look very similar regardless of their classification from minimum security all the way to super max. In Georgia most prisons can be easily recognized by their stone or brick facades surrounded by 20-foot high fences topped with rolls of razor wire. But close-security prisons have double rows of 20-foot electrified fences. Each row has several feet of razor wire at the bottom extending out about five feet and several rows of razor wire on top. The double rows of these 20-foot electrified fences totally encircle the prison. The fences are separated by 15-20 feet of open space with absolutely no vegetation visible. This is called the rabbit run.

The electrified fences are so sensitive that the slightest of breezes or the perch of a sparrow sets off an alarm in the main control room as well as in the perimeter car that circles constantly 24/7. The officer on patrol in the perimeter car constantly responds to alarms set off by the wind and birds. The double rows of fence also have six watch towers that are manned 24/7. The officers on duty in the towers have great views and approval to shoot to kill any inmate who does not stop while attempting an escape over or under the fences.

There are two entrances into RQSP from the outside. The main entrance, used by employees and visitors, is often referred to as the front bunker. The other entrance is the back gate and is used for vehicles making deliveries and crossing between main prison and the annex. Upon entering the main entrance, all employees and visitors must submit to an extensive pat-down by officers and pass their belongings through an x-ray machine. Also, they must leave their ID cards and personal keys with the officers working the front bunker; these would be returned upon departure.

Once people are through security, they stop at a reception desk inside the entrance to the main administration building and state their purpose for being there. Civilian employees continue on to their desks and offices. The uniformed officers, however, must pass through two more sets of electrically-controlled sliding steel doors before gaining entrance to the main prison compound. Here security is tightest. The first door must be securely closed and locked before the second door can be opened. It was at this point that it became imprinted on my brain that safety and security must always be on my mind. My life and those of my fellow officers would depend on it.

I mentioned I was excited and nervous my first day. But unlike a dreaded dental appointment, I couldn't call and cancel. I'm wearing a uniform and a badge. I'd better get real. And granted, I'm a morning person, but at still dark 5:30 a.m., it can make you feel as though last night just won't let go and allow you to pass on to your tomorrow. I made it safely to this darkened new day with all of the new things that await this newbie officer just beyond those gates.

I walked into the briefing and felt like the new guy that I was and took a seat at a table with an officer who sat by himself looking through some papers. He greeted me with his name, Barry Osborne, and a handshake. I introduced myself and settled in for my first briefing. As Barry was filling me in on how each morning briefing worked, he abruptly stopped speaking and turned his attention to the front of the room. The side door had opened and a tall, slender female lieutenant hurried in, carrying a large book with papers spilling out of three open sides.

Lt. Gwen Jackson got right down to business by telling the assembled officers to stand for uniform inspection. All stood at attention beside their tables that formed three aisles. Each sergeant took an aisle and walked down it, inspecting the officers' uniforms to make sure all were neat and worn correctly.

For those officers needing correction, their names were called out loud and clear with the infraction. OK. The uniform inspection was OK. But get this: we had to stand at attention with our hands outstretched, so our hands and fingernails could be checked for cleanliness. Is this elementary school? Insulting!

Once the uniform inspection part was completed, Lieutenant Jackson started roll call. When she called my name I was asked to stand; she told the group that I was the new officer to first shift and to please help me get acquainted with the ins and outs of everyday life at RQSP. Some people said hello, others nodded or signaled a hello.

To properly man all the posts of the prison it took at least thirty-five officers, but I could see that we were short of that number. I looked around and came up with twenty-seven officers present, not including the three sergeants and Lieutenant Jackson. How was she going to come up with the eight officers she would need to manage the prison and maintain proper security?

I would soon find out.

Jackson reported that two inmates who got into a fight during third shift were now confined to "C" building, the disciplinary lockdown building for general population inmates, until further notice. She reported on an inmate from the lower units who had been taken to Atlanta Medical Center (AMC) for self-inflicted wounds that were not life threatening. A team of two officers would have to go to AMC and relieve the two officers from third shift who were with the inmate.

When the report was finished, we got our assignments. When I heard my name called, I could feel my heart pounding against my chest. First-day jitters, I told myself. My first assignment in my new job was control room officer at the Annex.

The Annex was the part of the prison which housed inmates with relatively short sentences for non-violent crimes who were assigned to work on outside details. The officer supervised details that worked on contracted projects, such as maintaining and cleaning selected state and county roads, while other inmates were assigned to clean local, county, and state court houses.

I didn't even know how to get to the Annex. I learned fast, though. The best way to get there was to go back outside the prison and drive my personal car around to the back and park near the back gate and the guard tower. I drove along the sunken road which ran alongside the prison for about a half mile. I parked, took a deep breath, let it out slowly, and hauled myself out of the car.

I had to walk down several concrete steps to get to a metal hurricane-type gate topped with razor wire. To the left of the gate was a speaker and button. I pushed it, identified myself, and the gate was unlocked. I walked into the Annex for the first time. But my destination was the control room, and I wasn't there yet.

Blocking my path was an entrance with a Plexiglas double door with so many smudges and fingerprints that my one thought was I wouldn't want to have to analyze fingerprints from that mess. Ten feet straight ahead in the middle of the wide hallway was the elevated control room encased by thick Plexiglas. The control room was dimly lit, but I could see the officer inside and she could see me. She signaled me to come around to the other side. Before she opened the door she made sure the hall was clear of inmates. I finally had reached my destination—the small and stuffy control room.

I was to be Officer Brown's relief. Her unenthusiastic first words were, "If you are new, do I have to show you what you'll have to do and where everything is?"

I was saved by the bell, before I could say, "Well, yeah!" Brown answered the ringing phone. I could tell by her grimace that she wasn't happy.

She looked at me, ran her tongue over her teeth, took a deep breath, and then said calmly and pleasantly in something other than the king's English, "That was the lieutenant asking me to stay awhile and show ya what's happin' with the board and da keys and everything, cause you ain't never been down here before or anywhere else."

I guess I'm a fast learner, or at least looked like one, because Officer Brown was gone in an hour. Just two things sunk in: which buttons opened which doors, and which keys Sergeant Donaldson would chit out. Chit is a bronze inch round disk stamped with a person's name to be handed in when checking out equipment. This is an old state method of accountability and still used today. On my own, I learned that errors aren't tolerated and security and safety always come first and are never to be taken for granted. At the academy we were taught selfishness was a prominent characteristic in the criminal mind. How about lack of self-control? I saw that in action on my first day.

I was doing paperwork when someone started pounding on the glass of dorm 2 and screaming to let him out. "I got an appointment with the unit manager," he shouted.

I learned that first day that it's needless to get into a shouting match with an inmate. Just use the authority that comes with the badge and uniform. Like being a parent. You're not running for president; you're the boss. Same in a prison. The guy returned to his bunk in the large open dorm of fifty men.

Like kids, most inmates know that if they pound on doors and windows and demand things loudly and long enough, officers will respond by giving them the immediate attention they crave. I have my own problem—my temper. A strong control of my temper will be an ongoing battle.

Late in the morning I took part in the warden's daily inspection tour. Security's main concern for the warden is her safety when she enters each of the dorms. Her main objective is to inspect the inmates for proper dress, grooming and behavior. The beds are checked as well. They must be made to the exact standard set by GDC. Every inmate is given a photo of what the proper makeup of the bed is, and they must display this photo so it is clearly seen. The warden closely examines the floors and windows, the brass door handles, the walls for dust accumulation. Nothing can be out of place. Inmates will be held accountable for any infraction. The punishment could be anything from a verbal scolding to lockdown.

The warden passed through each dorm and spoke to several prisoners. She and her regular crowd of unit managers, senior uniformed supervisors, and several civilians finished the inspection in 15 minutes.

The next duty is the all-important noonday count. I had to make sure outside detail officers who took out work details this day filled out an out-count, which is an official Georgia state document that lists all the inmates' names and their respective GDC numbers, as well as their dorms and the name of the detail. This is important information when count is taken, because those inmates out on detail would be legitimately missing. Inmates counted as present will have their names and GDC number and bed and dorm assignments listed on the official count sheet.

Any first day is rough. Mine was no different, and I was ready for my relief at 2:15. Did I say 2:15? The second shift relief officer arrived at 3:45. What a way to run a business!

I had been told that Lieutenant Jackson wanted to see me when my shift ended, so I left the Annex, drove back to the main entrance of the prison, passed through security, got a full-body pat down and a full-body scan. When I got to her office, she had already left for the day. However, my trip through all the scanning was not for naught; she had left an envelope for me.

But even before I got to security, I had my first bit of excitement for the day. I was on a walkway when I saw a number of mental health inmates on a parallel walkway leading to the medical department. I noticed one of the inmates was holding something in his right hand that looked long and pointed. I immediately jumped the five-foot aluminum railing and grabbed the wrist of the inmate. I pulled his arm up and behind him and kneed the back of his knees forcing him to the ground with me on top. Several officers came to my assistance and cuffed the inmate and hustled him off to security to face the shift supervisor, Lieutenant Tuskey. I had to face Tuskey, too.

Tuskey was a guy of medium height, forty-something, shaved head, in shape. His first words were: "So you're

Wiles. Well, you have a lot of explaining to do on this one. I want witness statements from you and an in-depth incident report along with a DR (disciplinary report) for the inmate. Show me the paper work first so I can make sure you got it right. Now tell me what happened out there that made you respond like you did."

My confidence level was rapidly slipping.

Then he said, "Good job, man, and welcome to Rock Quarry."

That helped the confidence level. I told him what happened.

He explained that we both had an hour's worth of paperwork, and then I was on my own doing the disciplinary report.

I sat down to write my reports, which I would have to rewrite after Tuskey read them and told me how he wanted them changed, so it reflected what he wanted them to say. I made the changes; I didn't want to but I didn't want to look like I was hard to work with. Later there would be times when I would stick to my guns. No pun intended. Now was not that time. I patted my pocket where I had stashed the sealed envelope I had picked up in Jackson's office and called my first day — a day.

CHAPTER THREE

I sat in my car in the prison parking lot and ripped open the envelope and read a short note from an old friend.

"Welcome to RQSP, Wiles. I hope your first day was a good one and not too boring. In case you are interested in something more exciting than just babysitting these grown and dangerous men, let me know. I can sure use you in something that will be anything but boring; it may border on a little danger from time to time. Call me. Let's meet for coffee soon."

It was signed by an old friend of mine, Mark Thurmon. Thurmon was the chief investigator for the commissioner of the department of corrections and had been for several years. Before I entered the academy, we had met for a cup of coffee and he gave me an insight of what to expect at the academy and later while in uniform. And he asked if I would be interested in working on an important project with him when I completed my training. Now this note from him.

First thing I asked him when we sat across the table at Star-bucks was why would he want an inexperienced guy like me.

Mark looked around the restaurant, leaned across the table, lowered his voice and said, "Because this project is going to call for someone who knows how to keep things extremely private and not speak to others about it in any way, and that includes wife, kids, friends, and more importantly, your fellow employees. Maybe more important: you're brand new and have no other relationships at work other than me. Not one person at RQSP knows anything about you. That makes you perfect for this kind of assignment. And you got brains and the ability to understand and size up situations fast and accurately. Does that answer your question?"

I was stunned. And curious. Undercover? What is this assignment? What would I be doing? How would I be doing it? Who would I report to? How would we arrange for that to happen? Any danger? How much? Would there be backup and support? My questions would be answered — eventually.

On my ride home I had time to think. This was an opportunity. I could enjoy this work. I figured, though, that with undercover work I'd be in a difficult position at work. But I'd been there just one day, so hadn't yet made any friends with fellow officers..

Before I made a decision, I had to talk with my wife, even though I was told not to. Margie and I lived in a nice home in the suburbs of Atlanta about 35 miles from the prison, a forty-minute drive one way without traffic. We both liked our house and enjoyed living in this part of the city because we were close to all the good things that Atlanta had to offer, and we were far enough away from many of the urban problems. We wanted to stay put.

Before I entered the academy, Margie and I had talked a great deal about my career change at such a late time in my life and the impact it would have on our lives, both positive and negative. I felt I could handle the job. I work out strenuously with weights and run almost every day, and have for years. I had lots of energy and was in great physical condition and health for someone fifty-five.

If I were going to make a decision right away it would be to go ahead and do it. Of course, I had no idea how that decision would affect my life. Or should I say, the ability to hang onto my life.

CHAPTER FOUR

My day began at 4:30 a.m. A bowl of cereal and a cup of coffee, and I was out the door, It was a pretty easy thirty-five mile drive at that hour going north on I-85 because most of the traffic was going south. Of course, at 5 a.m. there's not much traffic anyway. The most traffic was in the parking lot. I wasn't the only early bird on first shift.

What I learned from these early birds, and from others at work inside the prison, was that so many of them hated their jobs and wanted to do something else. Maybe they'd quit complaining and leave. But in fairness, I understood the lousy job market, so they were stuck. And I was stuck listening to them day after day.

After the daily briefing, assignments were handed out. I expected to be back in the Annex, but no. I was assigned to building A with Officer Sherman, another newbie. Oh boy! Building A housed the largest number of the worst behaved inmates in the prison. I was assigned as the range officer and Sherman would be in the control room.

But what in the world was Lieutenant Jackson thinking when she assigned brand new officers to such a tough building? But the longer I was at RQSP, the more I realized how difficult it was just getting a body — any body — to man a post. The department was unable to attract and keep good officers who would be reliable both in attendance and ability.

Taking the range meant walking patrol on both sides of the two-sided cell block with two levels housing around fifty men in twenty-five cells on each side. I had no earthly idea of what was involved or what I was going to be in for.

Sherman was a young, attractive twenty-two year-old woman. Like me, she had just gotten out of the academy, and she had never worked a control room, or taken a count. This was going to be an important time for both of us. We would learn together over the coming weeks just how to run a building and always, always get the count correct.

If I were running the place, for sure, I would never have put two novice officers in the belly of the beast with no guidance. This was dangerous. The morning had just begun. Let's see how this would turn out.

A high security prison like RQSP is not a good place for on-the-job training. Inmates are aware of what is going on in their world and they know novice officers when they see them. Sherman and I were a gift to the inmates of "A" building. We were raw meat in front of pit bulls. We could have had some very serious problems. In fact, we came very close.

Dachon Fredricks, the inmate counselor for building A, was buzzed into the control room. He indicated a red book on a shelf and said that's where he signs in and out.

(Something new for Sherman and me to know.) "I'll be heading to the one side first then over to the two side. If anyone wants to see me, tell them I'll get to them as soon as I can."

I learned quickly that when inmates know that counselors are in the building, they queue up at the control room windows with requests to be speak with them. I went with Fredricks to start my rounds before first track. First track is the beginning of the day's main sanctioned inmate movement periods when inmates with a call out for appointments or other assignments are allowed to move outside their housing units.

Each day range officers get an accountability roster passed on from third shift, which lists all inmates in the cell block by bed assignment, as well as what each inmate has scheduled that day. These accountability rosters are the bible by which range officers of each cell block are able to manage the inmates assigned to their respective buildings.

Fredricks and I left the control room and proceeded through the heavy steel and glass door of one side of building A. The big door can only be opened when the control room officer mashes a button on the one side's panel and releases the lock. As soon as we entered side one, I could hear an inmate's voice boom out, "Look out for that inmate coming at you officer, he's bleeding pretty bad and has razor blades in his grip."

Sure enough, a razor-wielding six-foot plus inmate

staggered slowly across the floor toward me dripping blood from both wrists along his path. Fredricks stood directly behind me; I could feel a nervous hand on my shoulder.

"What're you going to do?" he seemed to choke on his words.

Good question. I surmised that his wounds were self-inflicted, which by the way, surmising is never a good idea inside the prison, but fortunately I was right this time.

I spoke calmly (no, I didn't feel calm) to the inmate and told him he was bleeding very badly and would need medical attention. The inmate looked as though he were gazing straight ahead and kept moving slowly toward us. The only defensive weapons I had were a clip board with the accountability roster on it and my two-pound Motorola radio. I decided they weren't enough. I would rather attempt to talk him into dropping the blades and getting down on his knees so I could help him get to the medical department. The radio did come in handy, however; I used it to call for assistance from any nearby officers. I refrained from using the 10-78 signal. Many of the working shift officers respond immediately no matter what else they were doing when a 10-78 call goes out. I didn't think I'd need the whole enchilada. (There I go "surmising" again.) But if I had made that call, the institution's operations would have been totally disrupted. To be honest here, I wasn't thinking about the total disruption; I just thought I didn't need to make the call.

The inmate had three inches on me and was as large as a bear, but he followed my instructions and got down on his knees. Once he started following my directions, I told him to sit on the floor and I would come over and help him. As I started toward him he sat down hard. The doors opened behind me and several CERT team members rushed in and cautiously put the inmate in leg irons. CERT stands for Cell Extraction Response Team, a highly trained group of five officers used for the most difficult tasks involving inmates. Each prison has one team.

I played Florence Nightingale and wrapped towels tightly around each wrist. The inmate was escorted to the clinic and a few hours later returned to the building extremely calm with bandages on both wrists. He went directly to his cell, lowered himself on his bunk, and stared at the ceiling the rest of the day. Whatever they gave him at the clinic sure made my day easier. I took a deep breath and... now what? I sniffed, and sniffed again. Marijuana. Like a bloodhound sniffing out its prey, I sniffed until I found the source. The lower range.

Let me set this up. In every cell block there are always guys outside of their cells doing any number of things. Some are chores like cleaning floors, some are leisure activities like watching TV, which is suspended eight feet off the ground. One of those guys serves as a lookout to sound an alert when someone in blue approaches. The alert was a loud yelp. But the yelp couldn't alert anyone which cell I was heading to.

This old bloodhound headed directly to cell # three. I yanked open the door and caught six-foot, 180 pound Darryl Bunckles with the stump of a lit marijuana roach in his right hand between index finger and thumb poised to flick his treat into the toilet.

Not on my first day, Bud. I thought and acted at the same split second and slid my clip board on top of the opening to the toilet. The marijuana stump landed on top of my clip board still giving off a little smoke.

Inmate Bunckles just looked at me and said light heartedly, "Ya don't think that shit is mine do ya?" I cuffed him, had him sit on the floor with his back against the wall, and told him to keep his mouth shut. To my surprise, he listened to me. I shook down his cell looking for more contraband, asked for supervisory assistance, and told Sherman to send all prisoners back to their cells and lock the doors.

I found a small clear plastic bag with a handful of grass in it. I looked over at Bunckles as I opened it and took a sniff. He gave me a weird smile, like he was caught with his pants down. "Bunckles, is this shit yours or are you holding for another inmate?"

"The shit's mine and I guess I'm fucked."

Mark Thurmon's job popped into my head. Maybe I could use this guy later. "Listen to me, Bunckles, if you help me I might be able to help you, what do you think?"

He answered me in half a second. "How can I help without being a fuckin' rat, which will do nothing but fuck me up. I gotta live in this place with these guys for a long time."

The laws of prison society. In the world of prison life, which is thousands of years old, there is the code of survival of the fittest and it applies in this jungle. The weak are preyed upon for everything from food to sexual favors. Rats only get hurt, or get dead. Even tough guy Darryl Bunckles lives in fear of going outside any of the laws. Lieutenant Jackson and two CERT team members took Bunckles to lock down in "C" building pending further investigation of the incident. CERT wanted to know who else was involved, and they wanted information to clear pending cases.

I had seen two other inmates leaving Bunckles' cell just before I smelled the pot and thought they should be pissed tested. Jackson told me the procedure to go through and the paperwork to file for this incident and the razor-blade incident, and that was that. Almost.

We got a radio message Warden Barton was about to start her daily inspection. The lieutenant stopped in her tracks right before leaving our area. This told Sherman and me that the warden was going to start her inspection with our building. And we sure weren't ready after our two "incidents."

Sherman looked at me with an "oh crap" look on her face. "I know I didn't get all the paperwork done while doing other things and handing out passes."

She meant she didn't document which inmates had exited our area for various reasons. And that meant we did not have the very most important thing for the warden's inspection – accurate inmate accountability. I was about to have a heart attack. I know I looked sick. " Gotcha!" Sherman handed me all the information we'd need for the warden.

Inspection was another education. The inspections team included Barton, Lieutenant Jackson, and six other people. The warden focuses on cleanliness. The inmates, properly dressed in their blue and white state uniforms, stand at attention in front of their cells. The warden enters each cell; beds have to be made according to standard procedure.

On this particular day, it seemed one inmate didn't get the bed-making memo. The warden walked into the cell, then back out, then stood right in front of inmate Byrd and let loose in "jailhouse language." Even my ears were burning. When the tirade was over, I was ordered to write up the inmate for a messy bed. Byrd attempted to respond to the warden.

She turned to me and said, "Add insubordination to the damn charges and if he says one more fuckin' word he'll be locked down."

I just nodded.

Her departing words were less caustic: "This is the best I've seen this building looking in some time; good job, Wiles."

I made rounds later and passed inmate Byrd's cell. I asked how he was doing.

"Why'd the warden get on me for such a little thing?"

I sure couldn't answer that one. Byrd couldn't even explain to her that he had just gotten off night shift working in the kitchen. And I sure didn't know that I was going to experience a great deal more behavior like this from Warden Barton, and not all of it would be directed toward the inmates.

One duty every range officer has is cell shakedowns, looking for contraband and getting rid of it. Contraband are items that the current prison administration does not approve of. These items could include anything that could be used as a weapon such as a toothbrush that has the plastic tip melted to a sharp point, or razors taken out of the plastic holders, or inappropriate reading materials, which includes all types of porn. A list of what is allowed and what is not is provided to inmates by GDC when they first enter the system from county jails. Which brings me back to Byrd. Byrd was working on something on his desk, which is the small metal shelf hanging from the wall. There, right in front of me, Byrd was making what looked like a perfect reproduction of a person's bank check. I snatched it up and looked closely at it. It was a perfect hand copy that could fool anyone. Byrd told me it was a made up name he used and he was just practicing. I took the forgery and knew that I should report it to Lieutenant Jackson, but decided to tear it up and throw it away. Since I didn't write him up as the warden ordered, I had two things I could use to bargain with Byrd for information now or in the future.

Byrd was one of the old school cons who had been around a long time and was in the know on almost everything that went on in his building and more than likely the entire prison. This would prove to be an important break for me and the investigation I was soon to be deeply involved in.

Inmates started to return to the building from their assigned work details or scheduled appointments. It was about time for the all important noon inmate count. All inmates returning to the building were held up at the sally port by control room officer Sherman, and not allowed back into the building until I could visually see them and make note on the inmate accountability roster. All the inmates who were in the building were then told to go to their respective cells and lockdown for count.

Every day without exception the start of the noonday count is announced with a broadcast over the radio. This was my very first noonday count in the role of building range officer and I admit I was very anxious. If I didn't have the correct amount of inmates on my accountability roster showing who may still be out, my building count would be off. I had looked over my roster twice before starting my count and was unsure if the numbers would square.

The inmates stood in front of their open cell doors; this is called being on line, ready to be counted. I slowly counted sixteen inmates on the lower range; my roster showed twenty-four inmates. Oh boy. I was missing eight men. Sherman made some calls around the institution to see who was on work details, or in prison terms, on out counts. Out counts are reports handed in by work detail supervisors (mostly officers) listing the names of inmates remaining with them through count time.

I repeated the drill on the upper range and counted twenty-six; my roster showed twenty-six. I was square for the upper range.

Now I had to see what Sherman had found out about our missing inmates. She found out nothing. She had called almost all the work assignments to no avail. And two officers refused to confirm if our inmates were with them. They told Sherman that if we couldn't get our information straight they would not help us out. What was that all about?

Once the count for a building is complete it was the practice at that time to call into the security office and give them the breakdown of what we had. It would sound something like this, "This is officer Sherman of "A" building. Our count on one side: thirty-nine men in and eleven out. Five at medical, six in trades for a total of fifty." That is how it would go if we weren't accidentally missing eight men.

Instead, this is what Sherman did say, "This is Officer Sherman and we are not ready to give our count because we show that there should be thirty-nine in, and we count only thirty-one. We can't find out where the missing eight men are."

I could hear Lieutenant Jackson on the other end of the phone, and she was angry. She ordered one of her shift sergeants to come and help with the count. Sergeant Wilcox arrived and took the count and got exactly what I had. It took the sergeant two quick calls to locate three working as orderlies and five working in the warehouse. Wilcox told us that the fault was not just ours, but also those officers who wouldn't tell us they had our inmates. Sherman called in the corrected counts and within several minutes it was announced that the prison count cleared, meaning everyone was properly accounted for. I relate this so you can see how important it is to keep track of the whereabouts of each prisoner.

Our relief was thirty minutes late, and then we were told to report to Lieutenant Jackson before leaving for the day. We knew we had paper work to do on the razor incident, the marijuana find, and the DR for inmate Byrd ordered by the warden during her inspection. But what now?

Sherman and I walked up the hill to the security office. I told her that I was not going to write the DR on Byrd and that I would take full responsibility if anything came of it.

We figured Jackson was going to give us a hard time about not getting the count right and holding up the clearing. Once the count is cleared, it is sent to the main office in Atlanta, so if there is a significant delay it could be a problem for the senior management of the institution.

Lieutenant Jackson is a tall black women in her fifties who has risen from CO1 to sergeant and then to her current rank. She has been a supervisor for over five years and the last two years has been the leader for first shift; she runs a tight shift. The problems that the supervisors have are due to the lack of dependability of the officers; they either don't show up for work, or they don't fulfill their duties once they are at work.

Sherman and I met with Jackson in the security conference room. She was enthroned behind an aged institutional gray metal desk. We sat on cold, hard metal chairs. Forget the cold part. We were in hot seats. Jackson let us know that she was very put off by how badly we did noonday count. I immediately spoke in our defense and reminded her that this was our first day; we had never taken count on our own before.

Jackson looked at me as though I had called her a dirty name and said, "I don't care. If you two are given an assignment as important as running a building, then it is on you to do it correctly. Do you two understand that?"

She took a deep breath and leaned back in her chair. "Look, I know you two are new; I wanted you to learn in "A" building, and then everything else at RQSP would seem a lot easier. Taking count is extremely important. Do you now know what to do tomorrow and all the tomorrows to come?"

Sherman and I looked at each other and nodded yes.

I realized that just about everything I faced at RQSP so far is nothing like I had experienced before. And I had just started! I wasn't in Kansas anymore. I had to follow the yellow brick road on my own.

Also, it began to sink in that supervisors at RQSP had no understanding of what their officers knew—or didn't know—about their respective jobs. I learned their attitudes were more about getting a job done and not how well it was done. As time went by, I would learn that this mind set existed all the way to the warden's office and was the cause of so many problems that affected the safety and well being of every person who entered through the front entrance of the prison. I had to remember that safety is always Job One and should always be the main focus of any prison's administration—and when it is not, the result is devastating to all who work within the confines of its reach. More about that later.

Sherman and I concluded our paperwork for the incidents that took place during our shift. "I guess you have good reason for not doing that DR for Byrd," Sherman said after we left the building.

I just nodded. I figured Byrd could be far more helpful to me knowing that he owes me. But I didn't want to give Sherman any inkling of what I would soon be doing for the commissioner's office. As I said, safety is Job One.

CHAPTER FIVE

Mark Thurmon set up a meeting in Atlanta for us with his boss, Paul Jacobs, the commissioner of the department of corrections. I wanted to know what I would be expected to accomplish. I would soon learn how all-engrossing a program was that I would be involved in.

Mark and I made our way through the glass doors of the outer office with Commissioner Paul Jacobs' name etched prominently at eye level. Jacobs greeted us and ushered us into his office. He closed the solid mahogany door and introduced us to the man already seated.

When asked to explain the history of how we arrived at his project, Mark related that in the past six months several internal affairs investigations had turned up information about internal corruption involving both civilian and uniformed personnel. Many of the IA cases involved smuggling of all types of drugs and all kinds of contraband, including cell phones.

After much detailed discussion between the four of us, it was decided that I would start working on the project right away. I would continue with my assignments at the prison, but begin to build a network of snitches to supply me with information to be used to root out the corrupting individuals. I would do this undercover, of course. I was assured by Commissioner Jacobs and Mark that all recommendations that I had would be taken seriously, and if it was critical I should act immediately with their full support.

We decided to put on the back burner a suggestion I had of putting an undercover investigator (UC) into the inmate population. The commissioner nixed my idea as being too dangerous to the UC. We decided to go with confidential informants (CIs).

Developing snitches, or CIs, is very time-consuming, and I was concerned that we might not get the type of information needed. But we were lucky; I did create some great snitches.

We talked of how to function as we move forward and the utmost importance of keeping the project in total secrecy. That was one big concern of mine—how to keep the project secret. Another was how I would be protected if things went sideways. I was assured I'd have backup, and by the time the meeting concluded I felt secure in my safety. Big mistake.

After the meeting, I stopped at Starbucks, ordered a black coffee, and used the quiet time to organize everything we had discussed so that I could feel more comfortable with this commitment. I had to convince myself this was the right thing to do. And then I had to convince Margie.

I took out my notebook and made a timeline. The idea for an internal investigation began when the commissioner became aware of an ever-increasing level of corruption among staff at several of the major prisons within the

Georgia corrections system. He met with Mark Thurmon, who is responsible for internal investigations of all parts of the department, for answers and ideas of how to put a stop to the activity. Mark and the commissioner developed a plan that resulted in my being brought into this latest meeting.

The commissioner's concerns focused on the effects corruption at this level is likely to have on the ability of his department to continue to perform safely and efficiently. Another of his concerns was the degree of outside influences over prison staff who may be involved with drug distribution within the institutions. And was this influence an organized effort or isolated to each incident? This would have to be a priority for us going forward and will prove to be the most difficult part of the overall investigation to substantiate.

The first thing the commissioner wanted us to look into, however, was sexual misbehavior on state-owned property within RQSP. We weren't looking forward to being the sex police, but when the commissioner asks, we do it. The commissioner had received some written complaints about Barton and he wanted to know it they were true or just disgruntled employees or jilted lovers sounding off. It was a "while-you're-at-it-take-some-time-and-look-into-this-for-us-and-get-back-with-what you-find" request, but "no rush."

But the first thing I had to do was talk to Margie. It wasn't as easy as talking with the commissioner. First, I had to convince her that I would be safe. Second, I had to convince her that I wanted to do this. At fifty-five, I didn't feel old. I was in good shape (not from genetics, but from working out). I had worked for the DOD in the US Embassy in Saigon as a high-level security contractor. So this wouldn't be my first ballet.

We talked into the night. I wore her down. She gave me her blessing. And I swore her to secrecy. (That kind of scared her; she almost expunged her blessing.) I never actually told her exactly what I would be doing, as Mark instructed, but I felt I had to let her know I would be doing "some" undercover work at the prison. I didn't tell her the full story until after I had been out of the system a few months.

The next morning I called Mark and asked if he could get me internal affairs reports pertaining to our "sex" project that would help me get started. He had already looked up reports; there was only one and all it could tell us was who was finger pointing (regarding sexual misconduct) at the RQSP warden. As I said, I wasn't happy with this type of investigation; it seemed like gossip, so I was relieved by Mark's advice: "Listen, Jeff, I don't think we need to put too much into this at first, maybe a little look-see and a short report. Then put it to rest, unless something significant shows up that we think would hurt the department or embarrass the commissioner if it became public. The corruption angle is our main focus, but if the boss wants us to look at it, we need to do it fast, then put it to bed."

At the time, neither of us realized how corruption and sex were intertwined.

CHAPTER SIX

Mark had suggested I transfer to another job in the prison where I would be able to move about without casting suspicion on me among the prisoners and, more important, the staff. I preferred to remain where I was until I understood how things worked at the prison, since I had only been there for two weeks.

Mark and I planned to be in touch every day with the state cell phone Mark had given me that has a shield that prevents it being picked up by x-ray when I enter the prison. I was instructed to keep it hidden and to use it only when I was sure no one could see or hear me.

A little background information here. In the hands of inmates, cell phones can be used to continue managing ongoing criminal activity; for example, inmates could arrange murders and prison drug deliveries. No surprise, then, that the corrections department considers cell phones contraband. No one, including all employees, is allowed to have them inside a prison. The exceptions to this rule are the warden, deputy wardens of security, and some outside law enforcement investigators.

So I used the cell phone shield to get through the x-ray machine at the prison entrance. But then I had to find a place to hide the phone on my body during the personal pat-down at the front bunker. Well, I figured that out. Before leaving the house each morning, I slipped the phone inside a plastic baggie and then inside my undershorts. As soon as I got through inspection, I would head to the men's room to remove my "contraband."

I knew that during the pat-down, most officers would rather not go near the genitals. I'm sure this was exactly how some contraband items made it into the prison in large numbers, either by corrupt prison staff or by visitors on inmate visitation day. While at the prison I learned how poorly educated and under trained some of the people staffing our prisons can be. The pat-down experience is a perfect illustration of this. With better training and proper supervision the amount of contraband entering prisons and into the hands of inmates would be greatly reduced.

At briefing each morning I sat with the same three officers and we'd gab with each other while waiting for the shift supervisors to begin our shift briefing. One particular older male officer, Jim Wallace, seemed to have taken a liking to me and had taken on the roll as my mentor.

Officer Wallace had worked at RQSP for over seven years and spoke often how he was looking forward to his retirement. Over time, Wallace confided in me about a relationship with a much younger female officer on third shift. Wallace is over six feet, has a prominent beer belly, and wears a badly rumpled, stained uniform. How did he get through inspection? He doesn't look like a professional law enforcement officer who is responsible for the safety and well-being of others. I would come to learn first impressions can be misleading and downright wrong.

My assignment this morning was to return to the much troubled "A" building, but this time with an experienced veteran, Officer Sharon Dade. As I walked along the walkway from the briefing on the hill to the "A" and "B" building security compound, I looked up and marveled at all the stars still visible. The 20-foot locked security gate had been buzzed open to allow me and three other relieving officers for the two buildings to go to our respective control rooms. Inmates were heading out to the nearby chow hall for the morning meal.

Dade and I made our way through the sally port and then into the control room of "A" building to get briefed by the third shift officers, and take over. Inmates stood by the large doors intent on going to breakfast. These guys are impatient when they are forced to wait before proceeding out of the building and onto the walkway that leads up to the chow hall.

We were inside the control room when a loud bang made us jump and duck. We turned to the window. Someone had thrown something heavy at the two-inch thick Plexiglas. Every inmate looked innocent; now there's an oxymoron. It was impossible to identify the culprit.

Dade and I discussed duties to get ready for morning count, which would take place when all the inmates had returned to the building from chow. I left the control room to start my rounds of each side of the building.

"A" building, like most other general population housing units, has two separate sides one and two with both sides having an upper range with 13 two-man cells and a lower range with 12 two-man cells for a total of 25 cells on each side. Our "A" building on this day had a total population of 100 men. It is the job of the range officer to supervise all that goes on with each man for the eight-hour shift. Trust me; it's not easy dealing with grown men who do not do well following rules.

The only weapon I had inside the prison, and the only link to backup was my communications radio, so first thing I did before starting out on my rounds was put in a new battery. The control room officer's job is to maintain a visual of the range officer and keep in constant radio contact. Dade is a seasoned veteran who knows the job and how to make sure we'd go home safely at the end of our shift. I learned so much from this fine lady in the many months we were teamed up together.

When all the inmates returned from chow, I'd make my rounds and make notes on the accountability roster showing which inmates were present and those who were not. Then Dade and I would compare notes; for those not present we would check the inmate's assignment and then place a phone call to that assignment to confirm.

This took a matter of a few minutes; we would then know who was where and be ready for the radio announcement to begin count. I would then go out and call everyone to attention and to stop movement, and then I'd count.

Once our building count was called in to the security office for approval, we would get ready for the mass movement of inmates—called session or track—to and from their daily work, school, medical, counselor assignments, or any place away from their assigned cell. A radio announcement is made once all the other locations reported their counts to security.

In the control room Dade and I would compare the notes and instructions for inmate appointments on the computer printout given to us at our earlier briefing. We'd note who can leave and to which assignment, then I'd leave the control room and step out onto the sally port in preparation of marking my roster as inmates leave. I'd look out onto the empty, calm compound with the morning haze just beginning to lift and the pleasant sound of chirping birds. Sometimes it is hard to believe that I'm locked away in prison with convicted felons.

On this particular morning, the inmates lined up quickly behind the large steel door waiting for Dade to press a button that will allow me to open it and let them onto the sally port with me. I give the OK to Dade to open the gate. As the inmates from side one rush onto the sally port, it is clear to me that I'm surrounded by thirty-five men in blue and white prison uniforms. I'm not usually nervous, but I felt uncomfortable until Dade released the lock to let us all out.

When the latch clicked open, a wave of men with their pent-up energy flooded past me so fast I didn't have time to assure each one was already marked out to an approved assignment. I learned that I must double-check to make sure inmates have an assignment before they are released onto the compound. I would learn there were many officers who did not check the inmates as they left the buildings and therefore, they were free to roam the compound. It goes without saying that inmates who roam can and will cause trouble. This is a perfect way of moving dangerous contraband of all types, as well as a means for getting at some unsuspecting targeted inmate.

There are inmates with dorm assignments as building orderlies. These are the guys who keep everything clean, from the shower, to the windows, to the concrete floors, to the—get this—the brass door handles. The warden inspects every day and she's a stickler for cleanliness. For example, if dust is in corners, any streaks on windows, any mold in showers, or a bed not tight enough for a coin toss, inmates would be in trouble, but so would the two officers in charge of the building. And, yes, this is the warden I have to investigate for sexual misconduct. Stay tuned on that one.

With inmates out on assignment, range officers make rounds on both sides of the building including upper and lower ranges and can do unimpeded random cell checks and in-depth searches for contraband. I always hit numerous cells during these rounds and often found insignificant contraband that I could use to later deal with inmates for meaningful information. There were times that I did come across a cell phone which had been poorly hidden inside a mattress, or a shank made from a sharpened toothbrush stuck inside the cell door jamb. The offending inmates were most often locked down in "C" building. One of the things most sought after during a shakedown of a cell would be any form of drugs or its paraphernalia.

When Dade and I were getting ready for the warden's inspection, inmate Lemuel Andrews returned to the building from his regular assignment on a maintenance detail. This was unusual.

Unless inmates had a prior appointment at medical or with their counselors, they stayed at their assignment. When I asked Andrews why he returned, he stammered, which was out of character for him. He muttered that he was feeling dizzy, so the supervisor let him return to the dorm to rest. I sent him to his cell, and said I'd talk to him in a minute. I asked Dade to check out his story with his supervisor, Sergeant Patt; she verified his story. She said she told him to return to work when he felt better. Dade and I looked at each other with puzzled looks. This did not sound right. What Patt should have done was send him to medical. This sergeant would turn up later in my investigation.

I went back to talk to Andrews. He stood near his

bunk looking through his metal wall locker and turned as I walked in and looked surprised to see me. I stood six inches from his face and looked into his very glassy eyes. "Andrews, if you are feeling so dizzy why are you going through your locker?"

Andrews looked at me like the little kid who got caught with his hand in the cookie jar. "I..I..I was looking for something to munch on."

I didn't believe it and wanted him to know it so I asked in an obviously suspicious tone, "Andrews, what is it that you do with Sergeant Patt over there at maintenance?"

"Painting classrooms over at the school; I think that's what made me dizzy." He sounded like a kid with a baseball bat denying a broken window to his father.

Unless I had him tested for marijuana by the CERT team, there was little I could do to act on my suspicions. But the last time I made a request, no action was taken. Usually CERT acts on its own suspicions, or they wait on orders from Warden Barton.

When I returned to the control room, I asked Dade about Patt, whom I had not yet met. With a sarcastic grin she said, "Patt is an ex-marine who acts like a tough drill instructor, and not only with inmates. She has been known to cross the line with officers she supervises. The odd thing, Wiles, is Patt is usually on second shift, so I don't know why she is even in the maintenance department now." Dade looked through some papers and held a sheet up in her hand. "In fact, according to this schedule she not only is not on first shift, she is not even on this rotation and shouldn't be working today. Let's see what she has to say."

Dade dialed and I could hear the ringing on the other end; there was no answer. We then called Jackson, our shift leader. Dade asked her if she knew that Sergeant. Patt was working in maintenance today. That was it; that's as far as Dade could get.

"What the hell are you talking about? Sergeant Patt is on second shift "C" rotation and they don't come back to work until our week is over on Saturday! I'm calling over there now and get to the bottom of this." Before she hung up we got our strokes. "Thanks for the heads up, you two."

This was my first brush with what would turn out to be an important find in my investigation, as I followed the import of drugs from the outside and how they get distributed inside.

Several days later while working with Dade in "A" building I kept close watch on inmate Andrews before he left for his assignment. Once he left "A" building for his job in maintenance he would be able to move freely to many locations doing whatever work was assigned to that specific crew. This freedom gave him the perfect opportunity to move and distribute contraband throughout the prison. Of course, he would give special attention to the most valuable and desired of all contraband: drugs. And the two most important drugs are marijuana and cocaine, with meth coming in a close third and growing fast.

Andrews, in his early 50s, had been in prison on and off most of his adult life. Interestingly, he seemed to always get the right job, be housed in the right building, and have a personal locker stocked with items that indicated he had a great deal of money in his inmate account.

The first private moment I got, I called Mark Thurmon for some answers. Besides the dollar amount in Andrews' account, I was interested in the deposit dates, who was making the deposits and if more than one person, and how often they repeated sending money. The answer to these questions would tell me if Andrews was involved, how deeply he was involved, how long he had been involved, and if we were extremely lucky, with whom he was involved. I would also be able to move forward with getting the next stage of the investigation set up. What I needed to know now was when another delivery from Patt would take place. When I had the information, Mark would then have the option of arresting Patt with drug possession on state property, or pressuring inmate Andrews to implicate Patt with information that could be used to force her to resign. The resignation part was a bone of contention for me and for Mark. The department prefers resignation or termination versus prosecuting to avoid bad publicity. This doesn't make sense. If someone breaks the law— and helps others break the law, namely inmates—that someone should be prosecuted, and not permitted to simply resign.

Now I needed to compile the information about drug movement I had gleaned from my observations and from reliable inmate snitches. If Mark decided he would rather arrest Patt while she was committing this felony, he would use uniform supervisors here at RQSP who were totally unaware of my connection. It would appear as though it came to Mark from inmate Andrews. With me out of the picture, I could keep my cover.

But this was speculation, as I still didn't have the information regarding Andrews' account. That would have to wait until I was off duty, sitting in my car and able to talk freely with Mark.

As the end of first shift approached, I prepared the paperwork to give to second shift. Most important is to have the accountability roster completely up to date and to have prepared passes that inmates will need to go to locations other than to their work or medical assignments.

It was always a relief when I got in my car at the end of shift. I had made it safely to the end of the shift, and home was a short drive away. I could now make the phone call to Mark to get Andrews' information. But I had another reason to talk with him. He had asked me to think of an assignment for myself in which I'd be able to have access to all areas of the prison. I found the perfect job: warehouse supervisor.

Mark had the Andrews information I requested. His store account was consistently kept at an average of $150, and every time he spent any money from it a new deposit was made with a money order from a different person each time. My guess was he was getting that money to pay for help to distribute contraband throughout the prison. I was confident that given the size of the prison and how it was broken up between lower units for mental health inmates and the upper units for general population, that Andrews would need other guys to help distribute his drugs. I had to learn how contraband moved around the institution and who handled it after it got inside.

The next morning at briefing, I once again sat with Officer Wallace. I listened as he complained about his much younger girlfriend who seemed to be losing interest in him. I've heard his story before, many times. And I'm tired of it, but Wallace is a nice guy, so I listened. Two minutes later, I sort of tuned him out, but then I perked up fast and became very interested in the rest of his story. The girlfriend, Gretchen Ford, was twenty-four and a sworn Georgia peace officer. She had worked on third shift at RQSP for the last several months since graduating from the GDC academy. When she met Wallace, she told him of her lack of accommodations. He offered his place at a very reasonable rate. She moved in right away. Four months later, and not getting anywhere with her, he wanted her to pay more rent, which she claimed she was not able to. And the reason? She owed money to her ex-girlfriend whom she lived with for two years before moving to Wallace's place.

The interesting part of his story was that he saw Ford speaking several times to civilian manager Arlene Kennerly. Kennerly is a forty-something openly gay woman originally from New England who lived in a double-wide mobile home she owned on state-owned property next door to the prison. The GDC made strips of land available so they could ensure the facility would have senior supervisors nearby in case of emergencies. Most employees don't like the close proximity to the prison, so to make it more appealing, the state doesn't charge rent for mobile home space, and often pays the utilities.

When I agreed to work with Mark and the commissioner to expose corruption at RQSP, they told me they had heard complaints involving Warden Barton and her after-hours behavior at her state-provided home. Even though these files are to be kept secret, I was in the need-to-know group and needed-to-know who was involved. Well, well. One of those people was Officer Jim Wallace. I now knew how to start my investigation into the warden's suspicious behavior.

This was going to be a difficult investigation because of the nature of the complaints and who was involved. I'd need to observe the warden for a pattern of behavior exhibited toward female officers versus behavior directed toward males.

CHAPTER SEVEN

Mark came through with the job. As the officer in charge of the inmate supply warehouse, I would be able to move around the prison compound without raising any questions from either inmates or staff. If there were inmates I needed to speak to in connection with an investigation, it would be simple for me to arrange a signed pass to come to the warehouse to pick up items they had ordered. This would not be out of the ordinary of the daily routine of the prison. The sooner I made the change, the better.

I found it necessary to speak with Mark several times a day. Before I moved to my new job as warehouse supervisor, I would often have to call Mark from the toilet/supply room inside the building control room. The officer sitting at the control panel was only two or three feet away and certainly could hear me speaking in hushed tones. I devised a silly scheme in an attempt to mislead the other officer so that she wouldn't question what she heard. I'd make up stories that I would let the other officer in on slowly, like, "I've had this crazy song rattling around in my brain since I woke up this morning," or, "I was rehearsing a little talk I was giving in front of a few guys from my book club." I think it worked.

Either that, or people thought I was crazy.

I got my transfer. I was now on split shift, 8 a.m. to 4 p.m. Split shift existed to reflect similar work hours to those in the department headquarters in Atlanta. Most officers on split shift had post assignments that required interacting more closely with the civilian office personnel and higher administrative staff within the department. Posts like inmate warehouse supervisor, maintenance supervisor, trade school officer, school and library officer, conducted their assignments during normal business hours of 8 a.m. to 4 p.m. Monday through Friday.

Immediately following my first split shift briefing as warehouse supervisor, I picked up my secure warehouse keys, cuffs, and radio at central control. The department uses chits, round brass disks, an old-school method of accountability to show who is in possession of items. Each officer starts the day with five chits, which are slightly larger than a 50-cent coin. They have the officer's last name stamped into it for ID purposes. I used three for my three pieces of equipment I would need that day.

The warehouse was just a short walk through two security gates, one which required an officer to buzz it open from a nearby control room; the other needed a key from the set I just received.

The warehouse is in a large steel building that also houses the food warehouse and the all-important and always dangerous chow hall. I opened the heavy steel door to the warehouse and passed into another sally port with another locked security fence that I opened with my new set of keys, then locked it behind me. I was now in the massive inmate warehouse with its row upon row of metal shelving reaching from the concrete floor to the 25-foot metal ceiling. Long metal lighting fixtures, metal cages protecting the bulbs, hung in rows of six from front to back and side to side. These lighting fixtures and their large gas light bulbs gave the warehouse a cave-like appearance. My office was in the back behind yet another locked chain linked gate. Three scratched and dented gray metal desks were crammed between seven-foot metal racks stacked with inmate uniforms and boots. I figured which desk was mine—the one with the telephone and computer, it was now 8:30, time for the inmate detail to report for work. I picked up my new (to me) phone and called central control and asked for an announcement to all housing units to send the warehouse detail to their jobs.

I had a list of the six inmates who were assigned to the warehouse detail. One of them was the only Georgia state trooper serving time in general population. Dee Matterson's case dated to the early 1990s and received widespread TV coverage due to his position in law enforcement in North Georgia. He had been convicted of sexual assault on a minor in a heavily publicized case, for which he claimed innocence. He had already served ten years of his thirty-year sentence and would actually get released several years later after years of court hearings. The other five inmates were David Doane, a murderer who had already served thirty years of a life sentence, Harold Vonn who was convicted of a non-violent white collar crime for embezzlement of corporate funds through phony checks, Jose Garcia for sexual molestation of his stepdaughter, and Ben Albright, serving twenty years for assaulting a friend while under the influence of drugs, Mike Zoller, serving forty-five years for armed robbery and aggravated manslaughter. A potpourri of crime and criminals.

The heavy steel front door of the warehouse was unlocked and only the chain link security gate was locked. This allowed all those needing to come into the warehouse only far enough for me to see and identify them. Being inside of a close security prison means always thinking of security first.

When the detail members arrived, I let them in and did a complete body pat down of each one to assure they were not bringing in any contraband and to set the tone with them; they would know what to expect from me. I introduced myself as their new supervisor and spent a few minutes finding out what their particular jobs were in the warehouse. Matterson acted as the inmate supervisor and worked at the desk next to mine. He had been on this detail the longest and knew the operation of the warehouse better than any of the other men. After I spoke with Matterson for awhile I figured I should be wary of him. With his knowledge of the warehouse operation, he'd be able to slip things by me. I'd learn that no matter how on top of matters I'd think I was, the inmate detail would still be able to get things by me; that was a fact of prison life.

Matterson told me that I'd soon meet Jane Robbins, a civilian from the deputy warden administration's office who was there as an assistant and to do much of the paperwork. And there she was. Jane Robbins, a young-looking twenty-something, came through the steel door and waited at the gate to be let in. She looked professional in a dark pantsuit and white blouse. Not only did she look professional, she was professional. She knew what she was doing, and it seemed she had the respect of the six inmates on the detail. But I wasn't too happy to have a young female in an area like a warehouse with six rugged male inmates who had not been too close to a woman in many years. But I guess there's a name for someone like me with those thoughts—chauvinist.

Robbins took matters into her own hands after our introductions. She said she'd help me get to know what is going on in the warehouse and how the computer helps get things done "in this crazy place." I told the detail to get started on their duties and not to give anything to anyone until they checked with me first. Then I tackled the computer.

Robbins had a lot of experience with inventories, shipping, and receiving, which is a large part of this job. She had been working at RQSP for just six months and I asked how comfortable she felt working around convicted felons. Not surprisingly, she said at first she was nervous, even though there is always an officer around. But then, she said, she relaxed and began to see the men as human beings and not monsters.

This was worrisome to me. I asked her to please not leave my presence without telling me—even when going to the restroom. The same about approaching an inmate within the fenced area. "Safety First," I said. "Anything or anyone make you uncomfortable, you tell me, is that a deal?"

"Right. A deal. Safety First."

The first incident that day happened twenty minutes later. Loud voices from the front of the warehouse by the chain link locked gate caught my attention. An inmate on the other side of the locked gate shouted at inmate Ben Albright, one of my detail guys. When the inmate saw me coming, he turned away and put his hands on the handle of the steel entrance door. I ordered him not to open the gate and to turn around and face me. He did exactly what I told him and then he spewed his venom at me. "All I fuckin' needed was a fuckin' pair of dem rubba' gloves so I can pick up all the fuckin' shit on dat grass and walkway, but your fuckin' guy thinks he's better den me and said he ain't got none. I know he's full a shit cause I seen anotha guy with some on."

Well, he did obey my command. After his tirade, I asked his name and told him to give me his ID card. Then I told him to lower his voice. Next, I told him when I opened the gate to come in and face the fence with his hands behind his head. He kept his mouth shut and did what he was told.

His name was Riggins and he said he was assigned to one of the mental health lower units and was told by Lieutenant Huskins of first shift to pick up yard trash. I told him we don't just give out rubber gloves because we don't have too many, and if he spoke to any of the detail guys like that again he wouldn't get anything but locked down by me. He nodded in acknowledgment; I asked Albright to give Riggins one pair of plastic gloves and told Riggins to say thank you when they were handed to him. He did. Incident over with no further action needed and several things accomplished. The most important was to keep something small from getting out of hand and possibly leading to injuries, the next was just as important: I demonstrated support for a member of the inmate detail when needed. I knew that some day this action was going to pay me back in needed dividends.

A call out went out to all the housing units. A call out meant that inmate passes had been issued to those who had warehouse orders to pick up. The completed orders are put in a clear plastic bag marked with the inmate's name. Sometimes this could mean just a few guys would arrive; other times an impatient horde would have to stand in line.

Whenever there is a gathering of inmates in one place, there is the risk of trouble due to gang or racial tensions, personal prison vendettas, or an instant flare-up of aggression caused by almost anything. I made sure that the heavy steel front door remained open while the inner chain link gate stayed locked, which kept the warehouse detail members and all other inmates separated in case of a problem. I positioned myself at the open window to pass the plastic bags through to the inmates. This way I could check their requests against what they actually would receive.

Inmate clothing items are in demand. They include: a white shirt with a blue collar with State Prisoner stenciled in black on the back, white pants with a blue stripe down the side seam, black ankle boots, blue knit cap, waist-length navy blue cotton winter coat with State Prisoner stenciled in white on the back, white cotton tee undershirts with State Prisoner in black on back, and white cotton boxers. Why the demand? They are considered currency of the highest value and are used to purchase food, services, such as cleaning of cells and clothes, and contraband from drugs to weapons.

As the inmates start to arrive, they line up in single file, which grows very fast and goes out the door and along the concrete walkway. There is another officer outside the warehouse who is monitoring the walkway movement and will also keep a close eye on things to prevent any trouble before it can kick off. The voices rapidly rise as the number of guys in line grows. The first inmate steps up to the open window and gives his name and building. One of the detail members stands next to me and gets the plastic bag off the shelf and opens it up to double-check the order sheet, gives it to the inmate to sign, then hands him the bag through the window as I watch. The first guy gets his bag, looks into it as he walks away and heads back to his building. This is repeated over and over again.

Then trouble started. A big guy with a shaved head, shirt sleeves rolled up showing large buffed arms looked into the bag and shouted: " I fuckin' didn't get what I ordered again, this shit ain't no good!" I quietly told him to settle down and we'd check his order. He told me that every time he put in an order he never got the whole thing. I let him inside the locked gate so we could speak out of earshot of the other inmates. (The main reason, though, is it's a good policy to immediately separate a troubled inmate from the others, so if things go badly there's only one angry guy instead of many.)

I looked at his handwritten order and compared it to the printout of what he was given. It did show that he was short a pair of socks, an XL tee shirt and 42 waist pants. We looked up his order on the computer and saw that his items were out of inventory. I let him know that the items were back-ordered and he'd get them when they came in. That problem was defused. I would learn that not all problems would be as easy.

Soon I would also learn what an important role the warehouse job would play over the coming months and years in helping me get the information needed to build cases against corrupt staff members. For example, the six slots for inmate warehouse detail were the most highly prized assignments in the institution and that any openings would sometimes start some very serious mini-wars in general population. Since prisoners don't have money, there must be some form of currency of value for trading in order to acquire certain things and services from other inmates. That currency is warehouse and food items. It goes without saying that anyone with access to the "currency" on a regular basis has power.

I realized that each of the six inmates on the warehouse detail used their job to enhance their status and create a much better life for themselves in the prison environment. Knowing this would be a very important tool for me in dealing with inmates who had what I needed the most—accurate information. I also could and would use my status as supervisor as leverage to get info by being the last word on inmates' ability to get goods from the warehouse.

Inmate detail member Jose Garcia knew his way around a sewing machine and would sit for hours repairing mattresses, pillows and some clothing. He would also make simple things like little cloth bags, which are considered contraband by the prison administration and could result in serious discipline for him if he were caught. I allowed him to continue to make these different things in his spare time, as long as he kept me in the know of certain things going on in his building. Dee Matterson got orders for certain clothing items that he would bring back to his assigned building and trade for food items and other favors. Inmate Harold Vonn also used the sewing machine to make and repair items he used to trade for things to make his life a little easier. Inmate Greybell would smuggle out toilet paper one or two rolls at a time toward the weekend because he knew it to be in short supply and in great demand.

Inmate David Doanes was a convicted murderer who had already served more than thirty years of a life sentence since he was sixteen; he was now forty-six. Doanes was the only one of the warehouse detail that didn't seem to have anything going other than just reporting for work and going back to his assigned building at the end of his workday. He said he had found God about ten years ago and that he needed little else to get him through. I never believed an inmate could be trusted, even one who had found God, so I kept a close eye on Doanes. I patted him down each day when he left the warehouse and never found a thing on him that did not belong to him.

The sixth guy on the detail was inmate Michael Zoller. This fellow was a whole long story all on his own. His thing was taking plastic garbage bags and trading them to guys who would fill them with water and use them in place of weights for working out. He was the guy to go to when inmates wanted new boots or long johns in the winter. Zoller became a reliable source of info on the power guys for the whites, blacks and Hispanics and their activities, as well as where things were hidden on the compound.

These six inmates would play an important role in helping me bring down some high-ranking staff who never knew they were being closely watched; they just went on about their dirty business until Mark Thurmon and I decided they were finished. We would decide that when we knew for sure they could not lead me up the ladder to someone else.

Jane Robbins was the one to kick things off when she told me that an inmate in the kitchen warehouse had made her feel uncomfortable. The large kitchen warehouse was directly adjacent to the inmate warehouse. The only thing that separated the two was another 20-foot-high chain link security fence with a barbed wire top and a locked gate.

I told Jane to meet me at central control where I picked up my keys, radio and cuffs, and we'd walk together to the warehouse. This way she wouldn't have to walk by herself among inmates who were on the walkways coming back from the chow hall that was in the same steel building as the warehouse. I waited one morning for Jane and could see her coming toward central control from the direction of the administrative area of the main building. She apologized for keeping me waiting, took a deep breath, looked around, and said, "May I confide in you?" We were on a concrete pathway. I also looked around to make sure no one could overhear us, then nodded for her to begin.

She told me she liked working in the warehouse and felt comfortable with the six guys in the detail. She said they treated her with respect and she never felt uncomfortable. In fact she felt as if they were looking out for her.

"Here it goes, right from the very first time it happened." She took a deep breath and spit it out. "After I'd been assigned here to the warehouse by Deputy Warden Pinsky to get the inventory problems straightened out, I started feeling pretty good about being here, and I'd talk to the guys on the detail and even the two inmates that work for Ms. Jefferson in the kitchen warehouse. Not really talk to the kitchen guys, but I'd say hi to them when I'd go over and talk to Ms. Jefferson and the older woman, Ms. Brady, who is her assistant. It became routine that I'd go over about mid-morning on my break. Ms Jefferson and Ms. Brady would share their homemade goodies and coffee and we would snack and chat.

"At first, one of the inmates, Cellors, from their detail would stop, get coffee and listen in on the conversation. In the beginning he didn't say anything, he'd just listen for a couple of minutes then go back to his duties. After a week or two he started adding to the conversation."

She paused, then said, "I know what you're going to say. The inmates always look for a way to take advantage of civilians. Especially women. But I know to be careful. But listen to this. I was sitting right here at my work area, and that gate that separates their part of the

76

warehouse from ours was not open, but when I looked up, inmate Cellors was standing right there trying to get my attention. I looked up and asked him what it was he needed, and he started talking about needing some new clothing items for a guy in his building who didn't have anything."

She held up her hands in the stop gesture. "I know, Officer Wiles, he was making it all up and that there was no other guy and that it was he who really wanted things. It was what he said after telling me what items were needed. He said that he understands that I'm young and cool and that if I'd get those things for him and did not enter it in the computer he could get me just about anything I wanted when it came to fun things like drugs."

She seemed to deflate like a balloon after she got all that out. Then she looked at me, held her hands out, and shrugged her shoulders, as if to say, "Now what?"

At first I was inclined to slap cuffs on the guy and charge him with sexual harassment and attempted bribe. Then the bell of refrain rang out loud and clear and I realized I could do something a lot better. I had no way of knowing at the time, but this information from Jane Robbins would be the impetus that would help me launch the four-and-a-half-year-long investigation that would involve many officers, supervisors, even the highest-ranking supervisors, and would include at least one murder and possibly a second some years later.

CHAPTER EIGHT

Emanuel Cellors is a guy that we all have read about or seen portrayed in films, you know, the one who spends more time in prison than out. Guys like Cellors, and there are many, thrive in the prison culture of survival of the fittest and damn the rest. Guys like Cellors have spent their entire young lives admiring, hanging out with, and emulating older guys, men who have spent their entire lives going in and out of prison and keeping the vicious cycle going.

Cellors first got sentenced to state prison for a domestic assault. Like all newbies in the state system he came through Jackson State Diagnostic Prison in Jackson, Georgia. He spent the first months learning the ins and outs of prison life that he had heard so much about from the older guys he looked up to as a kid. He learned on that very first night in the chain gang he would have to fight hard to defend himself against the advances of the well-established older cons. Fighting to protect himself would be an ongoing issue for him or anyone else that is young, short, and slightly built. He would learn that when he fights, even if he wins, he'd still lose. That's the way the chain gang sometimes works. If you win a fight, that's a challenge to the next guy wanting to strut his stuff. But if a fighter is caught by an officer, a disciplinary report goes in the file that follows him to every institution. He may get locked down in the segregated lockdown unit. In fact, many inmates begin their sentences just this way, and it can take a long time before things get straightened out.

This was Cellors' third trip to prison; he was an experienced convict. How he got the cushy kitchen warehouse detail is anyone's guess. But I was beginning to discover corruption within the system, so it wasn't hard to figure out. For certain, Cellors was trading food that he'd steal from the inmate kitchen and sell throughout the prison. He knew how large the building was that housed all the warehouses. He knew the many hiding places and how difficult it was to uncover something once properly hidden. But I knew he was able to get contraband like drugs for Jane Robbins if she just said the word. Too bad for Cellors that the word was to me.

Later Jane gave me even more interesting information that became an important piece of the investigative puzzle. Often while she was having coffee with Ms. Jefferson and Ms. Brady, Cellors would come in and either take something out or put something in the bottom drawer of the women's desk. She said at first it didn't strike her as wrong since she was unfamiliar with the routine or regulations of the kitchen warehouse. She figured she had no right to question how things were done. They kept the inmate kitchen and the warehouse functioning smoothly with very few visible hitches. It was the invisible hitches that concerned me. I admit I was aware that folks who have worked in the prison system around hardened inmates for years could take some things for granted and be taken advantage of. And I was aware that some put on a good act for self-preservation in the tense environment of the chain gang. And don't forget profit. They're doing the wrong things for the wrong reasons—profit.

To get Cellors backed into a corner I'd have to catch him in the act of putting drugs in the desk drawer. I would then have leverage I needed to squeeze Cellors for his cooperation, not to mention leverage I could use on Ms. Jefferson and Ms. Brady.

At the end of the workday in the inmate warehouse I would close out the computer and have the detail guys line up at the door in a single file. I'd do a thorough pat-down of each man starting with the top of their heads, hats included, to the soles of their feet, shoes and socks included. Each man would carry a plastic bag with items I allowed him to remove from the warehouse inventory so he could handle his "business" back in his building.

Why did I let them take items from the warehouse? They would then stay important in their buildings and stay important to me by giving me information. The information I was most keen on getting were the names of inmates or staff members who were expecting the drugs held by Cellors. If I knew when something was going to be handed off to him, I could move in. I'd just have to play a waiting game.

Mark Thurmon was going to feel upbeat about how quickly we were moving. Now what I needed from Mark was whether Cellors had a parole hearing looming in his future. If that were the case, I'd apply pressure on him for information and he would most likely comply. Information could make or break his chances of being granted parole.

OK. What I'm about to say now sounds like a bribe. The Georgia Parole Board looks poorly upon any disciplinary action taken against an inmate involving drugs. If I knew that Cellors was looking forward to a possible hearing date within the next year or two—you get the picture.

CHAPTER NINE

Several weeks had passed since I left first shift and started working at the inmate warehouse. I actually missed those 5:30 a.m. briefings and sitting at the table with Jim Wallace, listening to his tales of woe. He'd tell me how little sleep he'd gotten the night before because he and his young blond girl friend would get into fights and have hot makeup sex.

But the last time Wallace and I sat together it was different. Still the tale of woe, but the ending was different. No makeup sex. The girl was ready to move out. Wallace looked old and sad. He wanted to talk more, so we agreed to meet after work to talk.

We stood by my car in the parking lot. Wallace looked gray and haggard. His shoulders slumped, his five o'clock shadow stubbled, his face crumpled. Rejection's tough.

Wallace talked—and talked. In a nutshell, he said when Gretchen Ford (the young blond) had transferred from Hayes State, they got to know each other when he relieved her. She was on third shift, he on first shift. At the time, he was fifty-one, she twenty-three. Oh boy.

She had been living with a female officer from Hayes for two years. What Wallace didn't know until much later was that she and her roommate were hot and heavy lovers.

She had told Wallace that she didn't have a place
to stay near RQSP and had a long commute to work.
Remember, Ford was twenty-three and easy to look at, so
Wallace invited her to stay at his home. You know what's
coming: they hooked up. Wallace didn't know anything
about Ford's past liaison, but he was going to find out fast
and it would change his world.

Several weeks later Ford was suddenly being
transferred to first shift. Then Wallace told me the "rest
of the story." Ford had told Wallace that Warden Barton
often bumped into her when she went off shift in the
morning. Barton had told Ford that she enjoyed talking to
officers off the cuff. She would invite Ford into her office
to have a cup of coffee and talk about RQSP.

Wallace didn't catch any untoward meaning to
the meetings, but I did. I had a request from the
commissioner's office to look into complaints involving
the warden and her behavior with female staff.

Ford soon told Wallace that she wanted to continue
living in his house, but without "benefits." She offered
to share expenses, which she hadn't been doing before.
Wallace readily agreed because he figured he'd have time
to change her mind and they would again become lovers.
That is, until she told him about the romantic relationship
she had had with her female roommate at Hayes. And
she told him she had had other sexual relationships with
women and enjoyed them more than with men. Ouch!

During my daily phone call with Thurmon, I told him

about my talk with Wallace. His advice was for me to try to talk with Ford about her and Wardon Barton.

He mapped out for me what we'd have to put together before bringing anything to the commissioner's office. We'd need names of those involved, what they did, and places where activities took place. A signed witness statement would wrap it up with a bow on top, but that would be difficult to get. Who would sign their name to a legal document admitting to nefarious activities with the warden on state property?

"How about if we surreptitiously take some compromising photos to entice Ford or one of the others to sign the document? Then we could lose the photos after they sign."

Oops. Wrong thing to say, I guess, because suddenly Mark said goodbye and cut the connection. I figured he didn't want to hear about a bribe or lost photos.

I needed to make a connection with Gretchen Ford. I scheduled a warehouse delivery in her building. But first, I had another matter to attend to.

CHAPTER TEN

I arrived at the prison at 5:15 a.m. before first shift,
so no one would know I was there. I wanted to be in
position to see everything that went on in the kitchen
warehouse without anyone, even staff members, knowing
I was in the inmate warehouse. I had to see for myself
what took place when the inmate detail arrived for work
at 6 a.m. and how Ms. Jefferson and Ms. Brady related to
them.

All the warehouses, chow hall, laundry and barber
shop were housed inside one huge steel building. This
building played a vital role in the daily life of the prison;
therefore, it had a great deal of inmate and staff activity
almost twenty-four-hours a day. In prison, whenever
there is a great deal of inmate and staff movement, the
risk for trouble increases. These areas are known as flash
points for confrontations.

The design of this green metal monster provided
only two ways in and out when the truck delivery doors
on the loading dock were down and locked. People
entered through the main inmate entrance, which are the
front doors of the two chow halls A and B, or they entered
the way I did this morning through the locked steel door
in the clothing warehouse. I used a secure key, which few

people had access to and passed through several locked chain link gates. The laundry, barbershop and inmate store had their separate entrances and were isolated from the rest of the building.

In the inmate warehouse, we use a 15-foot-high rolling metal platform with stairs allowing us to get to the very top tier of shelves. The large platform had wheels that allowed it to be pushed by one person very easily, so I did just that to get to my vantage point on the top tier of shelves behind boxes shielding me from view. From up there I had a vantage point that allowed me to remain unseen from below, but gave me an outstanding sight line to every part of the kitchen warehouse including the freezer.

The first person I saw was Ms. Jefferson who came in through the main inmate entrance. She walked through the entire cooking and baking kitchens and was able to make sure the staff had the inmate detail ready to start the first meal of the day. It took a large number of inmates to prepare the three daily meals and serve them to the 1,000 convicted felons. Some of those 1,000 wouldn't be coming to the chow hall. For example, those confined to "C" building for disciplinary reasons have to serve their ordered time in lockdown, and mental health inmates must be monitored 24/7.

Ms. Jefferson unlocked the chain link gate to her office. There were several locked metal filing cabinets behind the two scarred wood desks. First thing she did was unlock her desk drawers and metal file cabinets. I heard singing, and it sounded great. In walked Ms. Brady, carrying several plastic and paper shopping bags. She dropped her bags on her desk, plopped down in her chair and sighed with relief. She had carried those cumbersome bags all the way from her car in the front parking lot through the front bunker security check, then all the way down the hill and through the front chow hall entrance. What of importance is in them anyway? I'd soon find out. She pulled out two casserole dishes of what looked like from my vantage point macaroni and cheese.

These women have worked together as the management team for the Georgia Department of Corrections Food Services division for over twenty-five years. They had worked in other prisons in Georgia and had been assigned to RQSP for the past eighteen years. They knew their jobs. They fed 3,000 plus inmate meals on a daily basis; they knew how to make a giant kitchen run and run well. Both had won departmental awards for having the most financially successful kitchens statewide, not an easy accomplishment.

But there was more to their story.

Ms. Jefferson, in her fifties, was smart, pleasant, and willing to help out when she saw the need. I liked her and hadn't met any staff member who didn't. It was a different story with inmates; they found her tough and demanding holding them to her high standards.

Ms. Brady was in her middle sixties. She was quiet,

soft-spoken, and never raised her voice or used curse words. The staff and inmates always followed her directions. I shouldn't have been surprised by the macaroni and cheese, since it was a known fact that she cooked up great food at home to bring into work for herself, Ms. Jefferson, and the rest of the staff.

I didn't like spying on these two women. I liked them. But I needed to know what Cellors was up to. Was he using the desk drawers in the office? What hiding places did he have?

I lay in wait on my perch. The inmate kitchen detail would soon arrive to get ready for the day's meals, and the peaceful quiet would turn into organized chaos as staff and inmates scurried in and out of areas currently locked. If anything was going to go down this morning it would probably happen by 7:30, before other officers arrived and the shifts changed.

I could see Cellors slowly walking in while talking to another inmate I didn't know. They seemed chummy and were laughing. As soon as they got close to the third-shift kitchen officer, they stopped their conversation and Cellors' chum engaged the supervising officer. When inmates engage in conversation with officers or staff members where there is a lot of convict activity, it is often to occupy their attention while something else is taking place. The kitchen officer's job is one of the most difficult and dangerous in prison because of the very large area to be watched over and the great number of inmates needed to run the kitchens.

Cellors walked into the kitchen warehouse and greeted Ms Jefferson and Ms. Brady in a loud voice. Ms. Brady directed him to get the hand truck and carry the bags of flour into the kitchen. As he worked, the "chummy" inmate with whom he talked with earlier showed up at his elbow. Cellors frowned and looked furtively around the warehouse. "Don't you know they can see us talking and they might wonder why? Here, help me juggle these bags now before they fall off the truck."

The chum said, "I need to get that stuff back from you, so I can give it to Scat before he heads back to the building, so hurry up, shithead!"

I could practically see fire coming out of Cellors' ears. But he said nothing. They delivered the flour and quickly returned. Cellors walked right past Ms. Jefferson and Ms. Brady without saying a word to them and pulled open the bottom drawer of the file cabinet and removed a large yellow mailing envelope with a fat bulge in the middle. He sauntered past the women without even hiding the envelope and headed out into the corridor along the loading docks and into the kitchen. I lost track of him at that point.

The women certainly must have known what Cellors was doing. He had gone into the filing cabinet drawers without asking and had taken out something stored there, then went into the cooking kitchen and disappeared. These two longtime employees of the department of corrections may not have known what he was keeping in those drawers, but they would know he was illegally keeping something in them.

I now had proof that Cellors was holding some sort of contraband and passing it to a runner upon demand. My next step was to identify the inmate runner—the chum. That was easy. I looked at the ID cards of those working in the kitchen. Inmate Damien Toban was the runner. I now had another piece of the puzzle.

Successful prison drug networks usually evolved into a layered structure with each layer serving a different purpose. There are the receivers or runners who get the contraband from the source as soon as it is inside the prison. The next step is for the runners to move the contraband very quickly to a holder, who then hides and protects the contraband until it is wanted. The runner then returns to the holder for the contraband and delivers it to the customer. It's a simple network, but there may be yet another layer, a distributor. He gets the contraband in bulk from the runner, then breaks it down into smaller amounts for sale to many inmate customers. The same drugs of choice bought and sold on the street are even more easily bought and sold in the chain gang.

Payment is made in many imaginative and creative ways. A personal service, such as washing and ironing clothes, cleaning a cell, or the very personal service of sexual favors, which tops the list. Any goods sold at the inmate store are used for payment, also. But the most sought-after prison currency are items from the inmate warehouse, including clothing, mattresses, blankets, pillows, and personal hygiene products.

Little did I know this was going to be the start of uncovering a large network that would eventually lead from the inmate holder Cellors, to a very high-ranking security supervisor above the rank of sergeant. I had no idea, though, how long it would take to unravel the network. And I certainly had no idea that I would get caught up in the net and almost lose my life.

CHAPTER ELEVEN

Later that day I worked without Jane Robbins' help. I spent so much time trying to make sure that I got every handwritten inmate order entered into the computer that I completely lost track of time. While I was engrossed in the computer, the inmate detail worked on filling orders entered the day before. I was interrupted by a visitor at the back gate. Inmate Damien Toban, the unidentified runner, the guy who was so chummy with Cellors early in the morning, leaned on the gate and flashed a wide smile showing two shiny gold teeth. "You sent for me?"

I told him I thought he could help me with something. His smile disappeared fast. To get him to come to the warehouse, I sent word that I had clothes for him to pick up. I unlocked the gate and told him to follow me. I couldn't make out what he mumbled, but I imagined he was worried. When you're doing something wrong, you never know when someone's going to find out.

I actually did have a package of clothes for him, but I also had a proposition to discuss with him. I handed him the bag of clothes and watched as he opened it and examined the contents. You would have thought the guy had just returned from shopping at Saks Fifth Avenue.

I made my pitch. "I hear you've been trying real hard

without any success to get a transfer out of RQSP to an institution in south Georgia; is that true?" I asked this in a concerned tone. The tone used between officer and inmate is often as important and sometimes more so than what is said. If the tone is accusatory or demanding, the response would be different than if the tone is understanding or conciliatory.

Speaking of tones, Toban's was full of disappointment. Quietly and slowly, he told me he had been trying to get closer to home. He said the trip is hard on his mother who is elderly and has serious health problems. He swallowed hard, his emotion showing on his face. "I been trying to get my counselor to help, but every time we talk all I hear from her is she's working on it and it will happen, but it takes time." The look of sadness and hopelessness gave way to a look of frustration and tension. "It's been two years of asking and still nothing. Officer Wiles, I tried doin' everything the right way, ya know by not getting locked down for anything in a really long time but still I get dragged and this shit has to change or I'm goin to explode."

I could see his whole body tensing up and knew it was time to make my pitch before he really did explode. Time to plant some seeds.

In a consoling way, I told him to stay cool and out of trouble and I would work on getting him transferred. If we were outside in the real world, two people coming to an agreement would shake hands, but in the chain gang inmates know they can never touch an officer or civilian staff. Touching an officer is considered an assault on a peace officer and would result in serious disciplinary action.

Toban is a smart man. "Why you wanna help me? We just met. There's something here I don't see, right?"

Inmates don't thrive in prison unless they are very tough or very intuitive and cunning. Toban had been in prison too long not to be suspicious that someone would help him without strings being attached. I looked straight into his eyes and said with conviction, "Right you are, Toban. If I can help you, there may be some way you can help me. First, go on back to work and think about how important this transfer is to you, then we'll talk more about it."

I learned two things: first, the transfer was extremely important to Toban, so he was going to give me what I needed, and second, I'd have to get him transferred from RQSP to south Georgia, pronto. I hoped he didn't take too long to make his decision; I wanted to strike fast so those involved would have no idea they were in jeopardy of being revealed. I needed Mark Thurman to set up the transfer. If I promised Toban he would be leaving, I had to be able to keep that promise.

CHAPTER TWELVE

Every day that I worked in the warehouse I'd get a radio or telephone call from a staff supervisor, either uniformed or civilian, asking me to fill a request for an inmate for clothing, boots, bedding, or extra personal hygiene items. Most of the requests from staff on behalf of inmates came as a result of conversations during the warden's morning inspection tour. The warden had a policy of not allowing inmates to receive replacements of anything beyond the standards that are received upon entering the prison system. There were exceptions due to loss, theft, or reasonable aging of items.

The policy was in response to inmates using clothing and bedding items as currency, therefore increasing the demand. In fact, the increase in demand became so great that inventory of such items as uniform shirts, pants, boots, sweatshirts, coats, hats, mattresses, pillows and blankets would be depleted long before another order from the state could come in. The state looked at every possible area to control cost, and inmate clothing and bedding supplies were targeted. Each institution received goods once a quarter according to the number of prisoners and no more, regardless of problems a lack of inventory would cause. There were very few exceptions allowed.

When I'd get a request, I'd check the order history of the inmate. If the inmate had abused the warden's policy and received more than the allotted amount of the items within a six-month period of his last order, the order would be denied. This could lead to tense moments and would require the intervention of numerous officers to make sure things didn't get out of control. As I said earlier, clothing and bedding are used as daily currency to buy items and services, so their value to inmates is great.

On this one morning I had sent the entire inmate detail back to their respective buildings to get ready for lunchtime chow call. Most often the detail was kept at the warehouse with me and would take a 15-minute break to go and get their lunch. This day was different because I wanted to speak to Mark about inmate Toban. I needed him to back up the promise to get Toban a transfer from RQSP closer to home as soon as he fulfilled his part of the bargain. Mark assured me that whatever I agreed to within reason the department would make happen ASAP. This made going forward a great deal easier for me; I could get done what I had promised.

Just as I hung up with Mark, a sergeant called me from the front gate; an inmate was with him. The sergeant's name was Jim Dotell and the inmate was Daryl Nochence from "A" building. Dotell said Mr. Major, the unit manager, told him the inmate complained that he needed new clothes. I looked the guy over and could see that from the torn leather boots on his sockless feet to the faded shirt that was years old, he needed some newer clothes.

I looked up the history on inmate Daryl Nochence. He had arrived at RQSP eight months earlier, and he got nothing from the warehouse except what he was issued when he arrived. In fact, all he got what was one used shirt and one used pair of pants, new underwear, socks and hat. Period. I asked him what happened to the other three shirts and three pants he had with him when he arrived at RQSP from Evans State Prison.

He looked at me with a kind of insane glare that I have only seen on guys in the lower units, the buildings housing the severely mentally ill inmates. I watched the guy closely, and asked Dotell to clarify that Nochence was indeed from "A" building. If Nochence was living in with the general population it was likely he was being taken advantage of by his fellow inmates. Prison is a jungle; predators prey upon the weak and it makes no difference what makes that victim weak.

Dotell seemed to agree with my thinking. "Counselors have no choice but to move some guys out of the mental health units because of no availability, but—." He just shook his head.

I put together an order of new and used clothes, shirts, pants, boots, socks, sweatshirt, undershirts, and pants and handed them to Dotell. "How long do you think he can hold onto this stuff?"

"I've already asked if he can be sent to one of the lower units buildings, "D," "E," or "F," so he'd get closer supervision and be less likely to become someone's easy patsy."

All Nochence did was nod his head, or look off into the space between the steel clothing racks and the chain link fence. I hoped he'd get moved to a lower building soon.

Another inmate headed toward us at a fast pace. He, too, was from "A" building and was sent by the manager. It seems his clothes were stolen as well.

Back to the trusty computer. I looked up this inmate's history. To do so, besides his name, Wally Times, I needed a Georgia Department of Corrections (GDC) number. Inmates carry an ID card with this information and facial photo on their person and visible at all times. I printed out the history and showed it to Sergeant Dotell and watched him read it and react. He looked down at Times, who stood at six-foot even and weighed about 190 pounds, and said to him forcefully, "You're kidding, right, Times? Mr. Major didn't send you down here. You came on your own to see what you could get. I'm calling him on the radio right now, so if he didn't tell you to come down here and ask us for this shit, now would be the right time to tell me."

Dotell took his radio and pressed the button, used his call sign and got the manager right away, and Major told Dotell to use the telephone in my office to call him. I watched Times as Dotell talked to Major; he looked nervous and unsettled. As Dotell listened to Major, his face got beet red with anger; this was going to get interesting.

As Dotell hung up, he took a deep breath, and said he was told by Mr. Major that he did not tell this inmate to go anywhere and he had not even seen or spoken to him today.

I showed Times the printed history: he had gotten clothes four other times this year. Times was agitated; Dotell was livid. He made a move toward Times and said very clearly, "Inmate Times, cuff up." This order meant that Times was to put his hands behind his back and prepare to get his hands cuffed.

Times started to back away from Dotell, but I was behind him, so he couldn't budge. Dotell, who is taller with a much longer reach than Times, grabbed his left arm with both his large hands and tried to bend the inmate's wrist in an attempt to move his arm behind him, but got stopped by a steel pole that was directly behind Times. I grabbed his right hand at the knuckles with my right hand and then struck the inside of his elbow with the clinched fist of my left hand and forced his arm to bend. I took my handcuffs and clasped them on his right wrist. Dotell still could not bend inmate Times' left arm behind him making it impossible for me to complete the cuffing. I then hit behind inmate Times' right knee with my right foot forcing him off balance and onto the floor on his face. Dotell brought his left arm up and behind him to complete the cuffing. I double- locked them for good measure.

Officer Shelly Edams heard the commotion, called for assistance, and came immediately from the adjacent chemical warehouse. The call from Edams brought the very large kitchen officer, Rowdy Hampton, within seconds of the call for assistance.

Both Dotell and I started to get up from the floor and off the inmate, then helped Times up. Suddenly he tried to kick Dotell's face. Officer Hampton brought him back down to the floor and brought the two us to the floor with him.

Just as suddenly Dotell turned and punched Times in the face, not once but twice, while Times' hands were cuffed behind his back. We all shouted at Dotell to stop. Within moments, Lt. Robert Greene and many officers arrived in response to the radio call of 10-78, the call for assistance.

The state's ten codes are used as a means of communicating information between people using hand-held radios. These transmissions between officers in dangerous environments are uniform and precise. The most clearly sensitive of all ten codes is 10-78, an officer's call for immediate help. Once a radio transmission of 10-78 is heard, all officers, no matter where they are or what they are doing, will immediately respond. One of the recognized problems with this type of complete response is how easily it would be to intentionally misdirect manpower, which is already dwarfed by the inmate population.

Lieutenant Greene took immediate control of the

situation and first established the condition of all involved in the incident, including inmate Times. He then asked two officers to escort Times to the medical department to be examined, and once he was cleared to take him to "C" building to be locked down. Prisons have disciplinary lockdown units, a kind of jails within prison, and at RQSP "C" building was for general population's troublemakers; "D" building was for mental health inmates who needed to be isolated for a time.

Lieutenant Greene told Dotell to make out his witness statement, incident report, and use of force report and have them finished and in his hands within an hour. Greene asked me to do the same reports as Dotell, but to do them separately and not to compare notes. He also asked anyone else who was involved with hands on the inmate to do the same reports and to have them done ASAP.

Officer Edam asked Greene if she could speak with him privately in her office, which was just a few feet away. I knew what was coming. She was going to tell him exactly what went down. No need for that; I was going to do just that in my written report.

The Georgia Department of Corrections spends a great deal of time and effort to explain the rules governing the use of force. For example, officers must de-escalate the use of force as the inmate lessens his resistance. Never is it permitted to punch or strike an inmate once he has been placed in restraints behind his back and no longer poses a real threat.

This case was going to be a problem for Sergeant Dotell. Internal affairs would investigate and report its findings, which would most likely result in disciplinary action, or even the loss of his job. I did not see the punches land, but I heard them and I saw the damage to Times' face.

Later that day during my telephone conversation with Mark Thurman, I learned that Dotell handed in his resignation when he turned in his reports to Lieutenant Greene, and it was accepted. Mark told me that Dotell had several complaints filed against him over the last five years by inmates. One of those complaints named two officers as witnesses to the problem. Dotell couldn't follow the law; how could he enforce it? In the course of my investigation, however, I would find myself up against other officers in Dotell's league. And some weren't mere sergeants.

CHAPTER THIRTEEN

Every Wednesday morning is supply delivery day to the nine buildings housing the overall population of inmates at RQSP; most weeks that would average 1,000 inmates. The supplies would be for individual inmates, but also for the daily functioning of the building including soap, deodorant, paper towels, toilet paper, plastic trash bags—big and small—and safety razors for those permitted to have them.

The inmate detail took about a half hour to load all these boxes and bags onto large, flat four-wheeled trolley trucks that they'd push in a caravan from one building to the next until we finished. I'd escort this little supply train to each building and have an officer sign off on the deliveries, so there was proof in case of complaints of insufficient items to last until next delivery.

This was a good time for me to check in at each building with the control room and range officers and catch up on what was going on in their location. It was also a good time to see some of the inmates I had developed a relationship with who could supply me with information. In return, I'd get them extra things they could use. I learned the system, didn't I?

Before we left the warehouse to start our deliveries one Wednesday, an inmate detail member, Jose Garcia, walked quickly right past me and placed something under a loose folder on my desk. "For when you get back," he said quietly. I acted as if I didn't notice anything, which is how he wanted me to react, I'm sure.

There aren't many different routes to take from the warehouse down to the part of the compound containing all the housing units, but I varied it as much as possible. This day I took the route that had as our first stop "A" building, which meant we came out the front warehouse door, turned right on the concrete walkway, passed the chow hall on the right, then turned left, walked down the slight hill past the inmate gym on the right, and stopped a few steps later at the chain link gate that opened onto the "A" and "B" building compound. All the gates that opened from housing compounds onto the main walkway had to be electrically unlocked by an officer sitting in a control room of one of the buildings on that compound, who watched who was at the gate.

Once we gained entrance to the two-building compound within a much bigger compound, we parked our carts and the warehouse detail checked the buildings' orders and placed these items on the enclosed sally port. I then went inside the control room and got signatures on the paperwork from an officer and afterward one of the buildings, stopping to speak to inmates. I'd check to see what items they needed, but mainly this was my opportunity to see if anyone had information for me. I'd handle this by walking around the upper and lower ranges, presumably looking for a particular inmate to sign off on a clothing item he submitted—a handy excuse to speak with that guy about something he had for me. On this particular day, I had payback. I had issued a new mattress the week earlier for an inmate and my good deed paid off.

Inmate Sandy Boggs was my informant with the new mattress. I learned that inmate Lemuel Andrews was selling dope this past weekend. I asked Boggs if Andrews got called out of the building either Friday or Saturday. "Oh yeah, he gets call-outs all the time from Sergeant Patt. Whenever he gets back from whatever they got him doin' everyone knows that it's party time for sure."

What was most interesting to me was that inmate Lemuel Andrews lives in "A" building as does inmate Emanuel Cellors. My suspicious mind wondered if there was something to these two guys being in the same building.

My detail and I delivered in "B" building, then headed down the hill to deliver to "C" building and the lower units. As I mentioned, "C" building is the disciplinary lockdown for general population, the lower units are "D," "E," and "F"; these three buildings house many of the mental health inmates at RQSP.

In order to get to "C" building and the lower units, we had to go through another locked gate that separates them from the compound which houses the general population. Outside of "C" building are totally enclosed steel cages for those inmates who are locked down and want to be outside for air and exercise an hour per day. The same arrangement goes for mental health inmates. Whenever anyone approaches the inmates in the cages, these inmates yell out all kinds of things from profanity to mundane greetings or information to be passed on to inmate friends. It is always a cacophony of sounds. In fact, it's loud almost anywhere in a prison because yelling is how guys will communicate over distances without the use of forbidden phones.

Usually the uniformed supervisor in the lower units would make special requests for clothing, boots, and bedding for mental health inmates. Most of the time the items needed were in the stockpile I kept of used clothing for just such requests.

One such supervisor was Lieutenant Roy. She had been on first shift in the lower units for longer than usual. Ordinarily, supervisors' assignments are rotated on a regular basis in the mistaken belief that this would eliminate favoritism toward posted officers as well as inmates under their command. In the case of Roy, rumor had it she demonstrated to administration an outstanding ability to work with very difficult mental health inmates. This was uncommon among other senior supervisors.

During this period, RQSP was under the stress of a lawsuit brought against the state of Georgia, the prison and warden by a mental health advocacy group on behalf of mental health inmates alleging they received practically no medical treatment by a poorly trained and abusive staff. The suit claimed to have sworn statements by inmates who witnessed the abuse and lack of treatment. This was one of the reasons that Roy was critical in these units; she was well trained for the job.

When I approached the cages of "F" building, I saw Roy just outside the sally port speaking with one of her inmate orderlies assigned to lower units. Inmate Ben Grumbly looked to be about 6'3" and 225 lbs. and in great physical shape; he was a great choice to deal with mental health inmates. When Roy saw me walk toward them she broke off her conversation and came to meet me.

Instead of a special request for a patient, she had one for inmate Ben Grumbly. She explained there would be a court-ordered visit the next day by the attorneys for the plaintiffs in the lawsuit and she'd like inmate Grumbly to make a good impression to show how professional RQSP is. Roy had a way to use her good looks to get most men to do whatever she asked. I was no exception. I told her to have Grumbly come by the warehouse and I'd fix him up. I was rewarded by her sparkly smile. She always made me feel as though there was something more behind her smile. But OK, I was smart enough to know that she did that with all men, and even with some women, and it worked.

Rumors in prison are different than in a normal workplace. Here there are two distinct cultures—inmate and staff. Rumors among inmates are hard to believe. Who knows if they're telling the truth, or if they're making something up to benefit in some way. On the other hand, it seems rumors about staff by staff might have some truth to them. And if rumors are spread by both inmates and staff, they just may be true.

The rumor I had heard several times from officers and inmates was that Roy was more than flirtatious with several male and female uniformed staff and in one case with an inmate. The rumor involving staff is nothing new, but a rumor involving an inmate is a very serious accusation. If true, it could cost someone her job and possibly a criminal charge. Frankly, to this day I think the rumors were bogus. I never saw any signs of unprofessional behavior of Lieutenant Roy with staff or with inmates; of course, her smile doesn't count.

On my way back to the warehouse with my detail, inmate Damien Toban headed my way. He handed me a signed clothing request for new boots. He told me he had a question about boot sizes. I knew what he really wanted was to speak to me and make it appear to others that it was about a boot request. I sent the inmate detail back to the warehouse entrance and Toban and I had a moment to speak privately. We turned our backs on the detail, in case there were lip-readers in our midst. Well, you never know.

I had been waiting to hear what he said to me: "I really need to transfer the fuck out of this place and get closer to home so my mom can see me more than once or maybe twice a year, so I'll help you in whatever way will get me the transfer."

To set this up, I asked him if he could get his brother to pay him a visit this weekend. We could meet in the shakedown shack on visitation day without suspicion. As soon as I knew the brother would come, I'd arrange the rest. I would be measuring him for his boots soon, so told him to let me know then if his brother was coming and, even more important, to tell me if something was going to go down beforehand. I told him to save his questions about the transfer until visiting day. I assured him, "It will happen very fast and very silently."

Toban had just told me that he agreed to help me with important information about the drug network within RQSP that involved not only inmates, but also sworn uniformed Georgia peace officers. I knew it took a lot of courage, even with the transfer, the reward he would get in return. The reward is why inmates turn snitch. It could be something that would make their lives easier or to avoid disciplinary actions. Damien Toban was turning snitch because he loved his family and especially his mother. He knew very well just how much his neck was on the line even when he got transferred out of RQSP, because these bad guys have a long and powerful reach and have no fear about using it.

Later, the inmate detail did their regular jobs. Jose Garcia worked on his pet sewing machine repairing a mattress; Dee Matterson operated the automatic labeling machine and glued preprinted cloth labels on clothing to be issued to inmates; Mike Zoller pulled orders and got them ready for pickup; and Harold Vonn repaired garments returned to the warehouse when inmates shipped out to other institutions.

While all of this was going on, I pulled a small sheet of

paper that had been placed under a file folder on my desk; this was called a kite. In prison terms, a kite is a note from an inmate to staff snitching out another inmate, or telling about something that is about to happen. In this case the note was from Jose Garcia. He wrote that inmate James Morris owned a working cell phone that he hid in a plastic baggy under a patch of uncut weeds at the left-hand corner of the sally port of "K" building. The kite informed me that Morris picked it up around dusk. It seems Morris was an entrepreneur; he sold three-minute calls every night right after he returned from working in the chaplain's office up on the hill.

Garcia's kite also informed me the word was out that a large volume of crystal meth was coming in next Friday. I folded the sheet of paper and put it inside the front cover of my work diary that I kept in my shirt pocket.

I had a decision to make. Should I keep this information to myself, or should I turn it over to the CERT team sergeant and let him deal with it. I often sent anonymous tips to staff members if I thought there was no staff involvement. But sometimes I was wrong about their non-involvement. If the staff was fast to act on the tip, fine. However, if there was no action at all, then I knew I was wrong. But not only that. Lack of action could have dire consequences. One time in particular an inmate was stabbed within an inch of his life because a member of the staff looked the other way. I decided the kite should stay with me; I would get the phone myself just before sunrise when I figured no one would see me.

CHAPTER FOURTEEN

A great cover for getting to work early is preparing for
an audit of warehouse inventory. Without a cover, I'd
have a hard time explaining why I arrived so early. Many
times I needed to get to work early to take care of my
"clandestine" activities. Since I didn't have to attend
the morning briefing, I merely picked up my security
keys, radio and handcuffs and was on my merry way,
and it was not yet daylight. I went straight down the
walkway through the locked chain link gate, and then
through another locked gate to the mini-compound with
buildings "J" and "K." I could see inmates through the
distorted Plexiglas, standing around waiting for the call
to the chow hall for breakfast. Wherever inmates gather
in large numbers there is an increased risk of trouble.
And the chow hall is one such place. To maintain control
over the number of inmates in the chow hall at any time,
the buildings are called one at a time. Once the inmates
finish their 15-minute meal, they are ushered out and
the next building is called. Most of the lower units, the
mental health units, do not come for meals; they have
their meals delivered by kitchen orderlies.

But breakfast wasn't on my mind this morning. I
headed straight for the farthest corner, the left side of "K"

building's sally port and took out my flashlight. Before I turned it on, I looked around and figured I was hidden from view. I spotted uncut weeds and stooped down and grabbed a handful. I almost fell on my butt, they came up so easily. There, in now clear view, was a clear plastic baggy lying in a dimple in the earth. And in that baggy was a black cell phone. I returned the patch of weeds to its original spot, pocketed the cell phone, looked around again to make sure no inmates or officers had seen me, and strolled back to the warehouse. The whole episode took maybe three minutes.

I would have liked seeing the look on inmate James Morris's face when he lifted up that plug of weeds and found his cell phone missing. I imagine his mind would be racing, trying to figure who in the inmate population would have known where he kept the phone and who would have had the guts to steal it. Morris had been down for a long time and seemed to be one of the more easygoing guys at RQSP. I said "seemed to be." In reality, James Morris was anything but. He was serving life for killing his father when he was 16 and was now in his 30s. He had many more years here. Men like James Morris do not survive the chain gang for over 20 years by being easygoing, and he certainly wasn't.

Back at my desk I called Mark Thurmon on my secure phone to set up a meeting to give him the cell phone for processing and to exchange other information. We agreed to meet during the lunch break at Wal-Mart, which is just down the road from RQSP. I'd call him when I was in the store and we'd meet in an aisle while "shopping." Most often these meetings took just a few minutes and then we'd leave five to ten minutes apart. I didn't think I ever looked like someone other than the warehouse manager at RQSP. Well, time would tell if I was right about that.

My next call was by way of the office phone. I called "A" building and asked to have Damien Toban come to the warehouse to be measured for boots. I needed to see him to find out if his brother would be coming on the weekend so I could set things up on my end. The excuse of measuring him for boots allayed any suspicion that he might be a snitch. A corruption investigation is sensitive especially when dealing with incoming drugs and solid information is what drives all the enforcement actions to follow. I needed Damien Toban.

Toban showed up at the chain link gate of the warehouse without delay. While my inmate detail went about their regular routine I measured his 9.5 size foot. I asked him in a near whisper if he was able to arrange a weekend. He nodded in the affirmative. "My brother's coming," he whispered. "My mom is too sick to travel. I gotta get closer to her."

I told him the plan for visiting day, all the while continuing to check to make sure the inmates in the warehouse were occupied with their jobs and not interested in our conversation. I told Toban I would be in the shakedown shack, the room where each prisoner is thoroughly searched for contraband—before visits—and after. He and I would be in there alone for a few minutes and we would then exchange information: my info about his transfer, and his info about transfer of drugs.

Then back to the boot business. As I walked him to the gate past the detail in hearing distance, we discussed his boot size: 9.5 without sweat socks, 10 with.

"Thanks. I guess a 10 would be more comfortable." With that Toban went through the gate I had unlocked and returned to his building. I felt like rubbing my hands together with a big smile on my face; but I didn't.

CHAPTER FIFTEEN

One reason I wanted to be assigned as warehouse manager was the ability I would have of using the high-value currency status of clothing and bedding to buy information. But another reason was the validity I could put on my travels to any place on the compound any time.

I left the warehouse for general population "H" building to make a delivery of paper towels, but for another reason as well. Jim Wallace's roommate and on-again-off-again girlfriend Officer Gretchen Ford was assigned there. I wanted to start a dialogue with Ford regarding her meetings at odd hours with Warden Barton. Maybe I could help Wallace a little, but I wasn't sure how.

When I reached the sally port at "H" building I was greeted by a striking young blonde woman. Officer Ford opened the sally port metal gate to let me in. She thanked me for the paper towels and commented that she thinks people must be taking them home.

I take that as an opening and tell her I think she could be correct because certain items don't last very long in the control rooms. I knew because when one shift ends and another begins I'd get calls asking for items that had been delivered earlier. Of course I knew I couldn't just come out and ask Ford what she thought of the warden and what her working relationship with Barton was like. So I merely asked her how the warden's inspection went for "H" building that day. She said it went well, "as usual." She asked me if the warden ever inspects the warehouse. Another opening. I smiled and said she doesn't and I'm glad. "If we had to prepare for a cleanliness inspection in a place that large we would never have time to get paper towels to you guys when you need it." I then asked Ford if she found the warden to be hard and not personable. She said without hesitation that she found her to be very pleasant and, so far, very willing to help her out whenever something had come up.

Warden Barton has a reputation for being far more interested in good-looking young females than males, so I could imagine Ford would find a receptive and welcoming mentor. I didn't ask for clarification of just what Ford meant when she said, "by helping me out when something came up." To keep the conversation flowing in this direction I said, "It's always helpful to have friends in high places."

Then Ford opened up. "Sometimes I wonder about her, because what I hear from other officers and other staff doesn't jive with how she treats me. One morning she was in her office when I got here early, and she gave me a very pleasant good morning and invited me to have coffee with her while I gave her my opinion about the difference between 8-,10-, and 12-hour shifts." "Maybe she has bigger plans for you, like a promotion to captain."

Ford laughed and said, "Yeah, I'll let you know when they give me those gold captain's bars. Thanks again and good talking to you; be safe."

As I started through the sally port gate I heard a call come over the radio that sounded garbled due to excitement but I could make out it was coming from "G" building, just a few short feet from me. I ran over to their sally port and could see the control room officer speaking on the phone and pushing buttons on the panel in front of her, all while looking over on the two sides and pointing at something. The sally port gate buzzed and popped open, and just as I ran in, Ms. Kennerly, the lower units manager at the time, and CERT Sergeant Damus ran in as well. Once we were all in the sally port, the control room officer buzzed open the side two door and we raced down the few steps to the lower range.

I'll never forget what greeted us as we got in front of cell 14 and looked inside through the small Plexiglas window. An inmate stood against the rear wall of the cell screaming, "Help me, help me," over and over, as though he'd seen a monster. Then we saw red smears all over the cell walls. We couldn't get into the cell. The heavy steel door had been jammed from the inside and we were trying to dislodge whatever was used as leverage. Through the glass we could see someone lying under a blanket on the lower bunk and blood pouring onto the floor. Hard to believe there is enough blood in a human being that could cover almost the entire floor of 6'x8' room.

Each one of us slammed our body's weight against the cell door, while the control room officer kept trying to electronically release the door in a failed effort to get the door open. We frantically tried to get into that cell to help the bleeding inmate before it was too late.

I couldn't tell who the person was that grabbed onto the steel at the edge of the bottom of the upper range walkway and swung his entire body against the cell door and kicked it in. The door opened and we rushed in; the screaming cellmate pushed his way passed us and ran out. CERT Sergeant Damus slipped and went down hard into the massive puddle of gooey blood. Kennerly and I rushed to the bunk; she grabbed a towel, wrapped it around the wound on his arm, then grabbed a second one and did the same on the other arm. I tried to get a radial pulse, then a carotid pulse without success. Medical personnel arrived and took over.

Once the medical team stabilized the patient, we helped put him on a stretcher for transport to the prison's medical center. We carried the stretcher in a rush out of the building to the waiting medivac golf cart. As soon as we lowered him onto the cart the medical team took off. An ambulance from Gwinnett County Fire Dept was waiting outside the medical center for transport to Gwinnett Medical Center in Lawrenceville. GDC procedure calls for two officers to accompany an inmate to the hospital, one unarmed in the ambulance, the other an armed officer in a following chase vehicle. I went as the armed officer in the chase vehicle.

As the armed officer, I was in the operating room with inmate Jason Dobbs while the doctors worked for an hour and a half to save his life. Later one of the surgeons told me those two towels wrapped tightly around his wounds saved him from bleeding to death.

CHAPTER SIXTEEN

Visitation is at a time and place created by the GDC; final approval of visitors is granted by the department of corrections. The hours are usually fixed for Saturday, Sunday and holidays from 9 a.m. until 3 p.m. During this time the inmates are allowed to have any reasonable number of people come to see them and they can spend part or all of the six hours visiting. Visiting day is a complicated process.

There are numerous officers assigned to monitor and supervise behavior by both inmates and their civilian visitors. Some visitors attempt to smuggle in contraband and they can be very creative and imaginative. The most common contraband is drugs and the methods used are unlimited, from inside babies' diapers and a woman's private parts, to inside bags of potato chips, or hidden between pages of greeting cards. Searching for contraband is very time consuming and should require special training, which few (if any) officers will ever receive before getting assigned to visitation. This means great opportunities for those bringing in the contraband to succeed with their attempts.

There are several key posts that are manned by the officers of split shift, which are the front desk, main visitation desk, roving monitors, and the shakedown shack. This last one is often referred to as the booty shack. You'll see why in a moment.

When visitors arrive, they must go through the front bunker and pass through the metal detector and get a cursory pat-down. They then proceed through the steel-gated sally port to the main administration building and the front desk. All visitors fill out paperwork in which they give their names and the names of the inmates being visited. When they are permitted to proceed they pass through yet another metal detector and go a short distance to a sliding steel door controlled by officers in the main control room who watch people coming in or going out. The officers then release the sliding door to allow visitors to step into a small area and wait for that door to close behind them before the door in front of them is released and slides open.

The visitors have now arrived at the large, well-lit visitation room, which has many areas of cushioned chairs set around small low tables. The tables are meant to keep the inmate on one side and the visitors on the other to prevent any touching after the initial greeting. Visitors present the paperwork to officers in the visitation room given to them at the front desk, which contains the inmates' names and location. The visitors sit and wait for the inmates to come up from their buildings, which can take awhile, especially if an inmate hasn't prepared for a visit.

That takes care of the visitors; now for the inmate

preparation. The officers in the visitation room call the inmates' buildings to let control room officers know of visitors for a particular inmate. The control room officers then make PA announcements in the respective buildings alerting the inmates that their visitors have arrived; in addition, the range officers make sure inmates are aware of their visitors.

Inmates having visitors must be properly dressed and then are allowed to leave the building. The first stop is the shakedown room, which is attached to visitation by a short hallway. Here inmates strip down to their birthday suits and each piece of clothing is examined for contraband and anything else not permitted to come into the visitation area. Items like watches are allowed, but must be listed by make and type to make sure the same watch leaves visitation with the inmate. Jewelry must be listed as well, to make sure it is the same when the inmate leaves visitation. They are then free to enter the visitation room. Once inmates leave visitation for any reason, they may not return.

My plan was to meet with Damien Toban in the shakedown room before his visit with his brother. The shakedown room is usually handled by one officer, unless that officer requests assistance due to heavy traffic to help speed things along. The GDC policy is to expedite the process so inmates and their visitors can spend as much time together as possible.

At 9 a.m. the first knock sounded on the usually locked

steel front door of the shakedown room, and an inmate orderly brought in the first of the visitation call-out forms to me. The inmate followed. I had left the front door unlocked so that I could let guys in faster and get them done, so they could get to their visitors and out of my way. I must have worked with at least ten guys before I got the call-out form for Toban from "A" building at 9:42 a.m.

When he knocked and entered, I closed and locked the door. We had a few short minutes before another guy knocked, so I wasted no time and got down to business. "Tell me," is all I had to say, and he started to do just that.

"Sergeant Patt brings the shit in most Wednesdays and Thursdays early in the morning and she gets Anderstone to meet her and he takes it to Cellors in the kitchen warehouse. Cellors hides it there in a drawer in the wooden desk."

While Toban talked, he started to take off his clothes for the shakedown. "Cellors then lets me know and I pick up for the "A"-"B" building compound; other runners that I don't know pick up for their buildings and then hand off again to another guy who is the seller."

I was about to ask several key questions when Toban stopped me by waving his hand and continued to talk. "I had gotta tell ya this now. There was supposed to be a delivery this past week and there wasn't. I was told that Sergeant Patt would be in Wednesday with a large amount of meth and weed. But there is a shortage down the hill because she didn't show and I been told that guys been calling outside to get some shit brought in during this weekend visitation."

He got all that out with no break for air. I waited a second to digest what Toban just told me about drugs coming in through visitation in greater quantity than usual to make up for the amount that did not show up earlier in the week. I asked him, "Would you happen to know what inmate or inmates might try to bring it in today or tomorrow?"

"I can guess but that's all it would be is a guess. Anderstone, Cellors, Childs from lower units, Briscoe from "G" building. Those are the only ones who might try that I know of."

I stopped running my hands over the clothes he gave me and told him to dress real fast. "Last question for today. How is payment done?"

"I was wondering when that question would come. Most times I pay when I pick it up from Cellors and the money comes from the guy selling the shit in the buildings. He gets it brought to him from two sources, one is during visitation and the other is from dirty staff. Most times I hand over about $75 to $125 to Cellors for each pickup."

"How do you get paid?" I asked.

"In store goods or services."

Just then an impatient inmate banged on the door. I opened the back door that led to visitation, and inmate Toban walked out and handed his paperwork I had signed to the officers at the desk. His next stop was to see his brother.

I took a few minutes to talk with Mark Thurmon and asked him to contact the shift commander for today, Lieutenant Tuskey, and tell him a large amount of contraband was on its way in today through visitation. Mark would give Tuskey the names of the five inmates involved. If those inmates had visitors today, we needed to check those visitors very carefully when they arrived. I would pay close attention to the inmates Toban fingered.

I was sure that I'd get a visit from Lieutenant Tuskey and he'd tell me as little as possible, since he wouldn't know I sounded the alarm about the incoming contraband. I figured he'd tell me to double-check the inmates more closely.

Whenever there was something of importance taking place that needed the help of multiple officers, the shift supervisors limited the information they shared. I had originally thought this type of exclusion was an attempt to limit the possibility of information leaking out and compromising the operation about to take place. I learned, however, that wasn't the case; it was the lack of faith and trust that supervisors had in their own shift officers. I would come to share a similar lack of trust and faith in far too many officers who worked alongside me. Unfortunately, I would learn the hard way.

There was a hard knock on the front door of the shake-down shack. "Officer Wiles, it's me, Tuskey, let me in."

I opened the door for Tuskey, as I finished my strip search of the inmate in the shack and let him out the visitation door.

Tuskey made sure both the entrance and exit doors were closed and we were alone before he said, "I just got word of the possibility that a large amount of contraband may be coming through visitation today."

I listened and nodded my head in acknowledgment of his words.

"Be real vigilant because these guys are real good hiding this shit; some of them have been doing it a long time," he said. "Make real sure that you check around the buttons on their uniform shirts and the waistband of their pants. Oh yeah, if anyone comes in here and says he's gotta take a shit, that's when he'll try and suitcase his stuff." Suitcase is when an inmate puts a plastic baggy of contraband up his rectum. If it's suspected an inmate has done that, he is taken to medical for an x-ray.

Tuskey told me something I already knew. "There's very little down the hill right now and this is replacement for stuff that never showed up this week. We might have a fight on our hands if someone is cornered." He rubbed his face with one of his hands. "OK, tell you what. I'm gonna assign another officer in here with you just in case something does happen, you ain't alone." Tuskey expected trouble.

My only concern was I didn't want one of those officers who take shortcuts. Tuskey looked straight at me almost like he knew what was on my mind. He would know it had to be a good officer not afraid of doing the job and the trouble that sometimes brings.

" Hampton, yeah, I think the best guy to work in here given the situation today is Hamp. I'll fill him in on what is going on. You OK with that?"

I sure was. Big Hampton was ex-army, well over six feet, and built like a defensive lineman at upwards of 275 lb. of solid muscle. I knew Hamp well enough to know he had my back, and he was never one to shy away from getting physical when required.

At 3:00 p.m. visitation would end, and all those who stayed until the end were straggled out the doors. Inmates would remain seated until then. They would then line up outside the shakedown shack and wait to be called in one by one. This was going to be a super slow process today and that always resulted with inmates getting anxious. Anxious inmates led to mouths running and sometimes more.

We had been lucky so far and all those inmates who'd left visitation earlier passed through very thorough strip searches with nothing more than some candy and a honey bun, both of which we had them eat before leaving. This more than likely meant that if any contraband was coming in it would be with someone outside our door. I had asked one of the floor officers, who normally would have left, to remain and keep close watch on the inmate line. Sometimes inmates will cause trouble as a distraction, and while our attention is drawn elsewhere they can get the contraband out during the confusion they have caused.

Hamp and I could feel the tension; we knew one or more of those guys had contraband somewhere on them. The cat-and-mouse game began as the first inmate came in and we closed the door behind him. Hamp stood in front of me and the inmate stood with his back to the wall that had the sink and toilet. We waited as the inmate took his time unbuttoning his shirt, like he was playing a little game with us. He handed the shirt to Hamp who stuck his arm out behind him for me to take it and go to work. I ran my gloved hand slowly down the front placket looking for any abnormality. Nothing. I rolled the collar and felt an uneven thickness from one end to the other, and when I turned the collar up I saw stitching that didn't look right. I stuck my finger inside and there it was—a folded sheet of plastic wrap. I gave it a slight pull and into the palm of my gloved right hand fell what looked like crystal meth.

I tapped Hamp on the shoulder and at the same time whispered in his ear what I just found, and that he should act normal and just continue. I wanted no trouble yet until we finished, in case this was an attempt to have us find the small amount while a larger amount would go unnoticed. I was pretty much blocked from the inmate's view so he did not know what I just found. When Hamp was going over the guy's pants we heard a commotion going on out in the hall. We both stopped what we were doing.

I pulled opened the door and saw Officer Jane Bard pushing an inmate's face hard up against the wall opposite putting handcuffs on his left wrist. Just as she was about to put the cuffs around his right wrist, he swung around so fast that his momentum threw her to the floor. I rushed the inmate as though I were making an open field tackle and slammed into the guy driving him against the wall and down to the floor face first. I put my right knee hard into the area right between his shoulder blades, grabbed the cuffs still attached to his left wrist and pulled up and over to meet his right arm. I yelled into his left ear not to resist, but he ignored my command. I punched him in his kidney area as hard as I could. He let out a loud grunt, went slack, and I slapped the cuffs on his right wrist.

As I got off the floor I told the inmate to remain there until I told him he could get up. Meanwhile, the officers from the visitation room were keeping the inmates in the line far from our little battle. Lieutenant Tuskey got the message about the scuffle and showed up within minutes. He asked if Bard and I were OK; we were. Then we reported what went down. The guy was put in a nearby holding cell, and I had a minute alone with Tuskey to tell him what I had found in the shakedown shack.

The two of us entered the shack to find that Hampton had done the smart thing by placing inmate Greg Sturgis in handcuffs to prevent anything from going down while I was out of the room. Tuskey told Sturgis that we had found the meth in the plastic baggy hidden in his collar and if there was any more we'd find it.

Sturgis looked at all three of us and said, "Hell no man, I ain't got no more fuckin' shit than what you guys already found." He no sooner ended his comment than I told him to sit down, and when he did, Hamp pulled his boots off his feet. I had one boot and Hamp had the other. The first thing I do with boots is remove the inner sole. As my gloved right hand pulled on the inner sole and lifted it out, there was a small folded piece of lined paper attached to the worn-out inner sole. I held it so that Sturgis could see it in my hand and then Hamp held up an identical-looking one. We gave them to Tuskey and he gently unwrapped them, making very sure not to lose any evidence. Both unwrapped little papers revealed tiny tabs of paper with what I'd guess was some type of synthetic tripping drug. When Sturgis removed his underwear he was told to face the wall and bend at the waist and spread his butt cheeks. When he did, Tuskey reacted fast. He grabbed the plastic baggy taped between Sturgis's butt cheeks. Quite a find. We found out later the plastic baggy held the most expensive of all the drugs we got that day— heroin.

We ended that day with a few more smaller finds, which resulted in four inmates being locked down in the disciplinary "C" building, including inmate Sam Polk, who I fought with in the hallway outside of the shakedown shack. I can't say for sure if we got the majority of contraband coming into RQSP that Saturday through visitation, but we did hurt those making the money and those waiting to party.

The information provided to me by inmate Damien Toban proved to be accurate and truthful and enabled us to stop a large amount of drug contraband from getting down the hill and into the inmate population. Toban's credibility would rise as he gave us more and more information that always proved to be accurate. Due mainly to his information, we were able to shut down a number of drug networks and, more important, rid the department of corrupt staff.

It was clear to me that I had to have another meeting with Toban soon to find out exactly when Sergeant Patt was planning to make her next delivery. I would then arrange for Mark Thurmon to interrupt her. If we could catch Patt with drugs in her possession, that would take this to another level and, we hoped, she would lead us to others.

I had other questions for Toban: How and when is payment made? Are Ms. Jefferson and Ms. Brady, from the kitchen warehouse, aware of the contraband being kept there? If they know, this could be a whole lot bigger, with far more sinister involvement than we thought.

When Toban answered one of my questions, how and when payment was made, I realized there had to be someone involved high up in the RQSP command chain. According to him, money was put into his inmate store account, which he then used to buy as many items as he liked. Then he used these excess store goods as chain gang currency to purchase anything else from drugs to other services provided by fellow inmates. He told me that as far as he knew, this was how the other runners and holders benefited as well.

Based on this information, I asked Mark to check the inmate accounts of those inmates we knew to be runners or holders. Two days later he gave me the answer. Cellors, Anderstone, Briscoe and Toban had similar amounts put into their accounts within several days of each other. But there was a complication. In all cases, the money was deposited by a family member or friend who had been making deposits like this for some time. In some cases amounts varied from just a couple of dollars to upwards of $100. I felt certain the smaller amounts were from the family or friend and the larger from someone who passed the money to the family to deposit in the inmates' accounts. That someone had to work inside RQSP.

It was the information on Patt that got us moving. Toban said he had been told to be ready because Sergeant Patt was coming Wednesday at 5:00 a.m. with a large amount of contraband and that it would need to be moved around to different locations as soon as it was in. This was perfect; it was the opportunity we needed, to be able to get a supervisory CO carrying into the institution a quantity of drugs greater than for personal use. Because inmate Toban had been so accurate up till now on everything he had given us we went ahead and made a plan to nab Patt.

Thurmon didn't want me in on the takedown of Patt. He insisted my involvement be unknown to anyone to protect me and to keep the integrity of the ongoing investigation. There was one supervisor Thurmon had come to trust at RQSP: Lt. Courtney Greene, and he would request his assistance with Sergeant Patt. I really wanted to be a part of the takedown, but I understood that we had too much to lose should I be found out.

Another question I had for Toban was how the dealers in the buildings paid for the contraband of drugs and cell phones they were selling. Easy answer. With cash. The money comes into RQSP by way of visitors and dirty staff.

It was time to make a transfer happen immediately and quietly for the very helpful inmate Damian Toban. At 10 p.m. he was safely transferred. The morning of the takedown of Sergeant Patt, I drove to work anticipating a call from Thurmon. I couldn't understand why I hadn't heard from him. He and Greene were going to be at the prison at 4:30 in the morning to be in place when Patt arrived at 5 a.m. I was nervous. Did Damian Toban give me bogus info? On purpose? I didn't want to believe that; he was so dead on with everything else he had told us. Maybe Patt didn't show just as happened the last time. I admit I was antsy.

As I turned onto Jones Church Road my state cell phone beeped. I answered immediately, my heart skipping some beats.

"We got her and she was loaded with contraband on her person and in her vehicle."

I must have been holding my breath; I started breathing as soon as I heard Thurmon's report. I was relieved. OK, I was happy. Not just for Mark and me, but in some strange way for Damian Toban as well.

We knew we had to get information from her. But if she fell on her sword like a hero and took the fall for fear of someone getting to her, we'd have a hard time getting any more than we already have.

Mark wasn't finished with his report and it was disturbing to me. The department was not going to prosecute; they only wanted her to resign. No fanfare. What a crock! What's wrong with this system?

Mark hadn't interviewed Patt yet, so we discussed a strategy he could use to get her to talk. He would let her think she would be arrested; maybe that would entice her to talk. Maybe.

So much for our strategy. Patt would only agree that she had in her possession crystal meth worth $250, marijuana worth $150.00, and a small amount of crack cocaine worth about $100. She agreed to allow her car to be searched and more drugs were found worth $1500. She would not give up the final destination for those drugs. Our best guess for the destination for the drugs found in her car was the RQSP Annex that was right behind the main complex, which housed all short-term non-violent inmates who qualified to go out on road details.

Patt was not fired, but did sign an agreement that terminated her relationship with GDC for good. While I'm still not comfortable with the easy resolution for the offending parties to drug smuggling and corruption, I do understand the department's desire to rid the culture of these kinds of people, without embarrassing publicity and legal expenses. But it still burns me.

Patt was gone, several inmates in the drug network were locked down, but there was an unresolved problem—how to handle the two women in the kitchen warehouse. Ms. Jefferson and Ms. Brady allowed drugs to be stored in the drawers of filing cabinets and desk while looking the other way.

CHAPTER SEVENTEEN

For years corrections investigators had information that right after a weekend of visitation and up until Thursdays there would be anywhere from $10,000 to $20,000 hidden on the compound for contraband purchases.

I would work another visitation very soon to look for some of this money that supposedly comes in every weekend. This was an ongoing problem and at every briefing, the weekend shift supervisors were to discuss with visitation officers from split shift the necessity and importance of diligently searching for money and contraband.

On that same subject, several times a year, there are large institutional shakedowns; the dates and times are kept from almost all corrections personnel, uniformed and civilian. The reason is obvious: to assure that inmates do not know what is coming and won't have time to prepare by moving or destroying contraband. Most of these large shakedowns involve entire shifts of the prison's officers as well as outside assistance from the department's highly trained tactical squad, which has hundreds of members. It's interesting and suspicious, though, that never are any large amounts of money or drugs found. There are always several cell phones, shanks, homemade alcohol, small amounts of drugs, and tons of pornography. This is all good to know, but not a bingo.

It is precisely these results from shakedowns that lends credence to the theory that there is someone much higher up in the prison chain of command who is corrupt and who leaks information in advance about such shakedowns, as well as smaller ones conducted more regularly. The person or persons behind this would only put themselves in such a dangerous position for some kind of personal gain. It was and is my view that this person is someone who is deeply involved with contraband smuggling for monetary gain.

Mark Thurmon arranged for a large shakedown of both warehouses the next morning. We knew what we would find in the kitchen, and did find. This gave Thurmon the reasons he needed to take both women up the hill to discuss their options. They both agreed to transfer to other GDC locations, and soon both used all the years they had accumulated and retired. They got off too easily.

When I started my shift in the warehouse the morning of the shakedown, I didn't have to do my usual early morning shakedown since a thorough one had already been done by an entire shift of officers and nothing was found. I called for my detail to report to work and I did the pat-down on each inmate. I then waited in my little office for weekend info to start trickling in.

First up was inmate Mike Zoller from "B" building. Mike was the type of inmate who was always a part of, or close to, most of the interesting events in the building housing many of RQSP's worst offenders. Mike came to RQSP from Valdosta State Prison after spending six months in disciplinary lockdown for being one of the leaders in an attempt at mass disobedience of inmates leading to a near riot. This put Zoller on a short list of inmates who needed to be closely watched, requiring Thurmon's influence to accomplish.

Zoller has so far not let me down about impending trouble between individuals or organized groups. Also, after a shakedown he'd know what contraband wasn't found, and where it was hidden. And he would tell me. Unfortunately, usually—not always— the goods are moved by the time I'm told.

This time when Zoller came into my office, he dropped two sheets of paper on my desk and walked out quickly. The papers were filled on both sides with information written in his handwriting. I started reading. I learned that not only was there no shortage of any kind of drug, but the same guys who usually pushed the stuff had been replaced by a new bunch of "entrepreneurs." There was no shortage of supply—crystal meth, crack cocaine, marijuana, and a fair amount of heroin. The supply would be available Friday afternoon. If they did run low, more would be delivered by an "A" building inmate during mutual yard time when everyone was busy speed-walking or watching other inmates play basketball.

Zoller's kite (the letter, recall, that informs on others) gave me information about inmate Billy Beagle, who is currently an orderly in the lower units working for Lieutenant Roy. According to Zoller's kite, it looked like Beagle was the guy making a lot of the deliveries and picking up payment. Interesting.

One major supplier, Sergeant Patt, missed making a delivery, and the fact that there were still so many drugs available was disturbing and showed me that there were many other players in this game ready and willing to play ball. To begin my investigation I wanted to speak to Roy about Beagle and, to be honest regarding the lieutenant, everyone was suspect at this point. When I learned she worked every weekend, you can imagine what crossed my mind. For sure I would work visitation the following weekend. But I wanted to see what I could find out before then.

My inmate detail and I headed out to make deliveries of clothing orders for the mental health inmates in the lower units, who are not permitted to come out to the warehouse without escort. Everything is on two carts in plastic bags with names clearly visible. We walked down the long cement pathway from the warehouse to the lower units and passed through large groups of inmates coming and going to who knows where; some have signed passes, but many do not.

This has been a problem at RQSP since I first got here. It always astounded me that so many inmates could walk around without a destination. Unsupervised movement of inmates is dangerous. For example, if the inmate population is alerted to an impending shakedown they could immediately move the important contraband to places less likely to be searched. What and where are those places less likely to be searched during a shakedown?

One of those places is out in plain sight, another is with dirty staff, uniformed and civilian, and another is underground, creatively hidden; still another is in the clothing and kitchen warehouses. Unfortunately, in all the many years I worked at RQSP, the warehouse had a proper shakedown only when I had insisted on it.

Once my detail and I reached the chain link gate we were to be buzzed in and then our little parade would proceed to the compound with "E" and "F" buildings and start making deliveries there. We'd gain entrance through another locked chain link gate that opens to the "EF" compound and my detail guys would start taking the plastic bags to the respective buildings and the CO's would distribute them.

I stood and supervised the guys as they took full loads of plastic bags to "E" building on my right. At that moment I heard a loud shout for me to come and help. I immediately looked to my left toward "F" building and saw figures on the sally port struggling; I took off running.

I had to yell to the control room to pop open the gate so I could enter. There were several officers struggling with an inmate who had his back against the steel bars of the sally port. The officers struggled to get the inmate to the ground. I jumped into help and had to get between the inmate and the steel bars of the sally port to apply pressure from behind to force him forward, then down to the ground. I got down to the ground close to his right leg as he continued struggling with enormous strength against the other three officers trying to get their grips on him. On the ground I found enough space between the inmate's legs and the steel bars to wedge myself in between and then with all my might I punched him behind his right knee. I could see his leg buckle slightly. I hit that same spot behind his right knee again; this time he almost fell, but not yet. I used all the strength I could muster and hit him hard behind his left knee; he grunted, but he wasn't down. He still struggled with the three officers hanging on him while the whole bunch stepped on me on the floor. I hit the guy once again in the same exact spot behind his left leg; this time he fell hard to his knees and under the sheer weight of the three officers hanging on, he went flat on the ground, breathing heavily. I hadn't realized the third officer was Lieutenant Roy; she did the honors and cuffed the inmate and slapped on leg irons before he again resisted. The inmate became extremely agitated again and started yelling. To my surprise, the inmate I'd been fighting with the last ten minutes was Billy Beagle the lower unit's orderly who worked for Roy. Interesting.

Beagle started yelling again. This time he was yelling at Roy. It was hard to distinguish what he was saying, but it sounded something like, "I could ruin your career, ya don't forget the guys who help ya when ya need it."

I grabbed Beagle on the left; Clemmons, a well-respected veteran officer and "F" building range officer, did the same on the right, and in a quick upward motion lifted him off the ground and started to move him away from the "F" building sally port and Lieutenant Roy. Beagle would have an extended stay in "C" building, no doubt.

I told my detail guys to wait for me; I'd be back over to get them in a few minutes. I wanted to ask Beagle some questions, and if we had privacy, I hoped he'd be candid with me. Of course the big question would be what he meant about ruining Roy's career. Also, I wanted to let him know I could get him out of lockdown fast and have him working for me in the inmate warehouse instead of lower units with Lieutenant Roy. I give for what I get. Beagle calmed down and shed his combative tone when he heard my offer. He was ready to cooperate as long as I added the incentive of quashing the disciplinary report (DR). Easy. A phone call to Thurmon and we'd have Beagle and his information about Roy and her corrupt dealings.

Lieutenant Roy was going down. Beagle told me Roy had him do a number of suspect errands. On her orders, he would deliver weed to certain mental health inmates who couldn't leave their buildings, and he'd deliver drugs like crack cocaine to general population guys who were locked down in "C" building. I asked him where she had kept the contraband during the recent institutional shakedowns. He said she kept the drugs on her person at all times and would only give the drugs to him when he was told to make deliveries. I assured him I would keep my part of the bargain and get him out of lockdown and into the warehouse. Beagle and his information were too good to pass up.

CHAPTER EIGHTEEN

Before my detail and I returned to the warehouse, I ran into Officer Ford, Wallace's "girlfriend." She was standing outside building G smoking a cigarette and gave me a limp wave in response to my robust one. When I spoke to her she seemed reserved and wore a frown. I didn't know if she was troubled, or just not happy to see me.

I debated whether I should probe, but, hey, that's what I do—probe—so I asked if something was bothering her. I hoped I could find a way to direct the conversation toward Barton.

She looked me and her eyes filled with tears. "Just things sometimes get overwhelming and I wish they could be different but they're not. I guess I have to learn to deal with it better, that's all."

I let her know I could listen any time she needed to vent. I left her with a "See you later." I had no idea how soon later would be.

I unlocked the chain link gate to the warehouses, laundry and school. The kitchen, chemical and supply warehouses, as well as the inmate laundry and barbershop are located in a separate metal building; all are in close proximity to each other. As my detail and

I approached the steel front door of our warehouse, I noticed what appeared to be a white envelope on the ground in a grassy area common to both laundry and warehouses. I pocketed it for later perusal.

Once inside the warehouse, I had a few minutes of breathing room. I began to realize how much I hurt from the incident with inmate Beagle. Something like that would never have bothered me in my younger days. I eased myself slowly down into my chair making damn sure I didn't anger my already pained muscles. If I were lucky and nobody came to the warehouse gate, I might be able to sit here without too much movement until after the noonday count.

I pulled out the envelope I had picked up; it wasn't addressed, and in fact had no writing on it all. I decided to open it and pass it on to the person to whom it belonged. I unlocked the drawer that contained my letter opener. Yes, I had to keep the letter opener locked up. I sure didn't want it go missing, only to be found in an inmate's neck.

I slit the seal and slid out two lined sheets of loose-leaf paper with neatly printed writing from top to bottom on both sheets. I started to read from the beginning and realized that what I had found was a love letter, and it was quite graphic. I didn't recognize the neat printing, nor did I know the person it was for, because the name used was obviously a love pet name. I got through the steamy parts to the end wondering if I'd find a signature. I didn't.

What I did know was that it referred to the numerous

times they had sex and the different types of sex they were having in various places of the laundry. This alone told me that it came from the only laundry/barbershop officer we had, Officer Rashika Crane, but so far I could not link it to any particular inmate. Officer Crane wrote how often she would call him at "K" building and all the different reasons she used for him to be sent back to work in the laundry. She wanted him to know how much their time together meant to her: she would do anything to spend time alone with him.

This is scary. Since this officer was willing to do anything for this inmate, how far would she be willing to go? Would she go so far as to cause harm to other officers or civilian staff? Crane had to be stopped and must lose her job before something serious happened to any of us.

Crane mentioned several times in her letter that when she called "K" building to have the inmate come to the laundry, he had just returned to his building from laundry duty—that could mean when they closed down for the day somewhere between 3 p.m. and 4 p.m. The best way to handle this type of officer corruption would be to involve the prison's deputy warden for security.

It was already 2:15 pm. First shift officers would be hoping their relief would arrive, or dreading the order to stay on for another eight hours. This happened a lot and no matter how many complaints were lodged, the practice continued.

Single parents felt the brunt of this system, especially if they had young children in child care. Not only did they have to pay for extra child care, but the state no longer paid for the extra hours worked. What does this mean? Simple. Lost income results in low morale and increased susceptibility to corruption.

I had been sitting at my desk mulling over the love letter when I heard a loud knock at the locked front door. There stood Officer Gretchen Ford. "Later" did turn out to be sooner.

I took her back to my office then rounded up my inmate detail, patted them down for contraband, sent them back to their buildings and locked the gates and doors. I was pretty much done for the day. Sort of. I still had the matter of the love letter, and now Ford.

She took a deep breath, let it out, and started talking. "Some things are bothering me. I might get into trouble just talking about them and being terribly embarrassed by my own actions." She had a hard time making eye contact with me. "I don't even know how to begin and I'm really scared of how it might end for me." If she had a handkerchief, she probably would have been twisting it in her hands.

I wanted her to feel comfortable enough to tell me what was troubling her, so I tried to assure her that I wouldn't repeat anything she said to me in confidence unless she agreed ahead of time. She seemed to relax after I said that.

She wanted to know how much I already knew

about her relationship with Jim Wallace, so she would know where to start. I didn't want to betray Wallace's confidence, so I simply told her I knew how and when she met Wallace and why she was living in his house until she found her own place.

Ford took it from there and told me that when she moved in with Jim Wallace he was so helpful with everything and seemed truly happy to have her living in the house. Jim would often tell her how much he enjoyed being able to sit and talk with someone in the evenings for the first time in years. She explained that everything went well until they had gone out for pizza one night and Wallace insisted on paying for it. Ford said she began to feel guilty at that point. And then Wallace showed signs that he wanted more than a roommate. "He tried to get me to drink more beer whenever we were in the house at the same time. I'm not stupid. I knew what was on his mind, and I told him I didn't want that kind of relationship."

She said Wallace agreed to stop pressuring her, but that didn't last long and he went right back to it within the same week. They were home watching a movie and having a beer when Jim got close and kissed her. One thing led to another, she didn't try to stop him, and they wound up having a night of sex.

Ford said after that she insisted that everything she did was to assure it wouldn't happen again. She admitted it had been hard avoiding Wallace, but she'd avoid him until she was able to move out of his house. "That'll be within the week. But that's not what's bothering me."

She explained that when she started working the first shift she arrived at work early to avoid Wallace at home. Warden Barton saw her coming in. At first the warden would say only good morning, then a few days later she asked Ford what her thoughts were about the possibility of going from eight-hour shifts to ten-hour shifts. That started up a conversation between the two that led to the warden inviting her into her office for coffee. "I was flattered the warden was interested in a mere CO1's opinion."

Ford had made a friend and that new friend was the most important person in the prison. She was back in the warden's office the next morning drinking coffee and eating Krispy Kreme donuts. That morning they discussed the importance of mental health training for officers who work in the lower units, even for those in the control rooms. These meetings and discussions continued over several weeks. Caron Kennerly, a unit manager, joined them once.

"Anyone else join the coffee klatsches?" I asked. Good question. I learned that Sergeant Patt frequented them until she resigned, as well as Officer Maggy Minton from first shift. Minton is a very pretty African American woman who should be modeling, making real money and not dealing with male inmates, who always get caught playing with themselves whenever she is near.

One morning, Ford continued, Minton stopped her after briefing and said the warden wanted to see her before she left for home that evening. Minton told Ford the warden had a "pleasant surprise" for her.

The surprise was an invitation to join a group of women from RQSP at the warden's house on Friday evening to discuss things of concern to them. Ford thought it was a great idea for her to meet with other women who work at RQSP and share mutual concerns with their caring boss.

Barton's home is a nicely kept, small three-bedroom, red brick ranch just across the road from RQSP. Many of the prisons in the Georgia corrections system have homes on their properties for a warden's use as a residence at no cost. Because of the on-the-premises residences, wardens were never more than a couple of minutes from work. This was important in the event of an untoward incident at the prison.

Ford arrived at the warden's house admittedly a bit nervous. Here she was in the warden's home, and she didn't know the other two women very well. Once she settled in and got comfortable with the other two—the recently resigned Gwen Patt and the good-looking new head counselor Justine Morgana—she felt a lot better and began to enjoy herself.

Ford told me that as the evening wore on and everyone had several glasses of wine with their cheese and crackers, things got a lot more relaxed and business turned into stories and jokes. Seeing the warden every day as the boss in a tense working environment, and now watching her relate to others in a private way, was a bit of a shock. The warden was very friendly and relaxed, laughing and telling jokes, talking music and families. Later, she started showing some interest in speaking closely and quietly with Justine Morgana, and that is when Ford took that as a signal to call it a night and go home. This type of gathering took place two more times, once more at the warden's home and the next time at Caron Kennerly's home.

I told Ford that I didn't hear anything that indicated she should be concerned about, or anything that could lead to trouble. She didn't have to worry about socializing with her supervisors as it was after hours and her time is her time.

She interrupted me and said, "I just gave you the background so that you'll see things in context and better understand what I'm saying."

What I heard next changed everything from this point forward for us all.

CHAPTER NINETEEN

The next gathering of the RQSP "women's club" took place at the warden's house, which I mentioned was on state property. This time when Ford arrived she was greeted by loud music and the same group, but they had been drinking before she got there. She said there was no talk of things relative to work; it was all laughing and dancing with each other. Wine, red and white, was flowing freely and at some point in the evening someone had turned the lights down low and lit candles to improve the atmosphere.

Ford had thought it would be another easy night spent with women who shared interests in their working place. What she did not expect was a pure social event that moved in an unexpected direction. The warden was dancing and snuggling with Justine Morgana, who didn't look too happy about it, while Caron Kennerly was working her way over to Ford with a big grin of determination. The other two women, Gwen Patt and Maggy Minton, were kissing each other on the other side of the now-darkened room.

Kennerly danced her way over to Ford while sipping her wine and slowly licking the rim of the glass. Ford started talking of their respective interests in football and track and how they both enjoyed going to see games and meets in person. She said that at some point during their conversation they both looked at one another, and then someone's closed-fisted hand came between them feeling each of them softly on their breasts. Then the fist opened, revealing two oblong pills. Gwen Patt kept her hand on Ford's chest, caressing it and told the two of them to go ahead and take them for a great time tonight. Kennerly told Ford that if she wasn't interested in it, that's okay, "but you're really going to miss a lot of fun and maybe some great sex."

I stopped Ford at this point and asked her if the pills were taken by any of the others, including the warden. She said she didn't know, but by their actions later on, she thought they probably did.

Actions later on? Kennerly and she talked, danced and drank wine; the others disappeared for a time and when they reappeared they were dressed in very skimpy underwear. The remaining lights were put out completely and from then on it was moans and movement, while she and Kennerly started getting caught up in the scene as well. I told Ford I didn't need any more details.

I asked her why she was telling me all this. Did something happen to make her afraid? Oh, yes. The warden talked to Ford the next day and told her she had better not say anything to anyone about what took place at her house. Barton told her that if anything came out she, Ford, would pay a serious price for shooting off her mouth. The others were prepared to deny anything took place; it would be her word against theirs.

There was more and she was scared. Patt and Minton told her they'd beat the shit out of her if they learned about anything getting out, even if it wasn't from her. I told Ford to go to work as if nothing happened. She had my word this wouldn't get out. (To myself I said, "Yet.")

"I'm scared, but not enough to look the other way." She gathered her things and stood to leave, then had more to say. "The warden's having sex and drug parties at her house," she said with a stubborn look, "and I'll help to stop them."

Why would she risk not only her job, but her well-being? She had the answer and my opinion of her rose.

"She's using her authority to get women to do drugs and have sex. I think they are going along with her because of her position. That's the reason I did it." She lowered her eyes at that statement. "I'm so ashamed."

CHAPTER TWENTY

This day wasn't over for me yet. I unlocked the gate for Ford and saw Roy heading my way. She looked serious and determined. Roy has stopped before to shoot the breeze by bragging about her latest escapade at her favorite watering hole in Gwinnett County with her gal pal Lt. Gwen Jackson. I admit, they are fun and stimulating conversations, especially when she gets graphic about her young pickups. Now what?

"Wiles, what have you got in here I can give to inmate Giles Murphy in "E" who can't keep from wetting the damn mattress?"

I told her to get a form from the guy's counselor, and I'd give him a coated mattress we have for the grown bed-wetters, of which RQSP has many.

She walked around the warehouse and scanned the many aisles and rows of steel shelves stacked to the 25-foot ceiling. She finally got to what she really came in for. "This place is so damn big, you need the tac squad to help you do a decent shakedown. Have you spoken to Mr. Tomley about getting in here and finding all that shit that's been hidden away for years?"

"I have. He says it's just too big and complex and agrees he needs the tac squad the next time we have a large institutional shakedown. That'll be sometime in about six months or longer. We'll get it done then." I gave it a little BS coating, hoping she'd bite now and not later.

She followed me into my office all smiles now and sat in the chair facing my desk. It was probably still warm from Ford. Roy is a cute woman and reminds me of that kid on the brink of getting caught doing something bad.

"Hey, if it wasn't for your inmates this would be a great place to hide Christmas gifts; did you ever think of that? Then she said something that made me sit up and take notice. "Hey, Wiles, you're the only one who gets the security keys for this place, right?"

Now we're getting somewhere. I answered in the affirmative and held up the large key ring with all fourteen keys and jingled them just to highlight their size, weight and number.

She shifted in her chair. "Before I say something, will you promise not to repeat it and keep it between just the two of us?"

This could be the link to her thinking that she is pulling me into her web. I agreed. (I'd add it to Ford's secret.)

"Do you ever think we get screwed on salary for the type of work we do, the risks we take every day working in this kind of environment?" Her expression showed how serious she was about the subject.

"All the time." What I didn't say aloud was that corrections make $10,000 less than other branches of law enforcement, and it shows in the type of people we attract versus those in other branches. So many of our people skate on the thin ice of incompetency and dishonesty.

To sweeten the pot of discontent, I said aloud, "It bothers me when I think of how hard we work and the dangers we face day in and day out. The low salaries are one of the big reasons we have so damn many officers looking to take second jobs. Or find something to make some much-needed extra bucks."

Roy cut to the chase. "Would you have an interest in making some of that much needed extra bucks? Yes or no?"

I was taken aback at how quickly Roy got to the point of her visit. Okay. I'd play along. "I guess it sounds inviting on the surface but I'd need to know more, like how do I earn the money and how much money is at stake?"

She must have anticipated the question, because her response sounded rehearsed. "Allowing me to come in and put things in a safe place could be worth $100 to $150 every two weeks." She held up a hand in the universal stop sign. "Before you say anything, there isn't anything that would or could hurt any of us. What do you think?"

My first question: "What do you want to put in here, and where do you plan to hide it?" Roy flashed a triumphant smile, then wiped it away. She thought she had grabbed my greedy interest and was close to closing a deal.

"I won't lie, Wiles; it's a small amount of weed for some of the mental health inmates. You can know where we hide it; I know you won't touch it. If it's found, you can act as surprised as the rest of us."

The rest of us? The rest of us sounds to me like there are far more uniformed staff involved in these drug networks than I had thought. This conversation really motivated me even more to find out who the rest of them were and to put an end to their careers.

"I guess what bothers me the most is having it found and then playing dumb. I don't think I'm good at something like that." Now that's BS. In this job, I've learned to be a pretty good actor. I stayed in my role. "How can you be so positive there is little chance the stash would get found?" I figured that was a question someone going into a deal like this would want answered.

"Because we will know in advance of any institutional shakedowns coming our way, or if any smaller-shift shakedowns are gonna happen." If Roy had swaggered, she wouldn't have seemed more confident. "Feel better?"

"So, there is someone higher up in the chain of command than you who is in the know about shakedowns and when they will happen, and that it'll get passed to us in a timely manner." I seemed to be pondering the thought. "I want to know who's going to have our backs. I want to know how secure I'll be."

I guess this wasn't Roy's first rodeo; she knew when to shut her mouth. She smiled and shook her head. "Sorry. Can't tell you, because I don't know myself."

"Then I'll have to decline the offer, but if you find out

later that you can trust me then let me know; I'll be ready. I'd like to know whom I'm involved with on something this sensitive." I stood and walked to the door to give the impression I really wasn't interested in discussing this any further, while silently congratulating myself on my acting skills.

Roy smiled at me and said, "Wiles, don't repeat anything we talked about, or you could be unhappy with the results. Bye for now."

I walked Roy out through the gates and returned to my desk, sat down, took a deep breath, and let it out slowly. I now had the answer as to how inmates always seemed to know in advance just when shakedowns were coming, so they could move and hide large amounts of cash and drugs before the teams arrived. I was now sure there were people much higher up in the command structure than shift supervisors. I thought of all Roy had said. She had no idea how she just helped my investigation. What I wasn't thinking about is the veiled threat she gave me. I shouldn't have dismissed it.

CHAPTER TWENTY-ONE

I closed up the warehouse for the day and went to see Brian Tomley, the deputy warden of security, to show him the letter I had that appeared to implicate an identifiable officer and an unidentified inmate from "K" building. In the pecking order of prison life Tomley's position is the next most powerful position in the institution after the warden. The deputy warden is responsible with anything to do with security, and that's what prisons are all about.

Tomley was on the phone when I got to his office and signaled me to have a seat. He ended his call quickly and turned his attention to me. He's a friendly guy—sort of a gentle giant type—tall, with a growing girth, dressed in a tailored business suit, and so polite. But he knew his business.

First thing he did was thank me for taking over the troubled warehouse. Of course, he didn't know I requested the job to help my investigation. Next comment: "My secretary said you wanted to see me about something of importance you found."

He opened the envelope and slid out the pages. He took his time with the letter then put it down before making any comment. I thought he would thank me for bringing it to him and then politely dismiss me. Instead, he asked me what I thought about the letter and how I thought it should be handled.

Tomley didn't know me or what kind of officer I was, so I was surprised he'd ask for my opinion. But he did, so I gave it. I told him I thought it was from the laundry/barbershop officer, Rashika Crane, and an unknown inmate from "K" building who worked in the inmate laundry.

Tomley seemed uncomfortable with a situation involving one of his female officers and a male inmate whom she supervises. I wasn't very comfortable myself. In the business of corrections this type of situation, between male inmate and female staff member always ends badly. The severity of just how this would end may very well be determined by how it was handled by the DWS.

"I do have an idea," I said. "We could find out who the inmate is by asking the control officer on duty at the time to see who returned from the laundry work detail then got called right back out again."

Tomley looked at me, then nodded. "Good. Would you handle this? I have to be away for a few days."

This was strange. Instead of passing it on to CERT, which normally handles all investigative details for the warden and DWS, it was passed to me. I wondered why. Lots on my plate now. I called Mark Thurmon to let him know what was going on. First I told him about information I heard from several of my CIs about a possible inside hit put out on someone. I hesitated to put much credence on the rumor as there was no inmate named as the target.

Mark said someone turned in a kite to the CERT office

that also mentioned a possible hit, but it, too, had no inmate name associated with it. When several different sources produce similar news, it can be the real thing. Needless to say, we were concerned.

Next, I told him we had a witness, Officer Ford, who was very close to making a formal witness statement and complaint against Warden Barton for sexual harassment and the unauthorized use of state property to commit a felony. We both agreed the case would be stronger if we had Officer Maggy Minton's statement as well.

I worked on Minton. I told her we had plenty on her drug smuggling into RQSP with Lieutenant Potter, and all we wanted was a signed statement detailing her unlawful activities with Warden Barton. She signed the statement quickly. Was Barton disciplined in any way? Hardly. She was transferred to Atlanta; there was absolutely no fanfare when she left. She retired shortly after the move.

Next up: Roy. I told Thurmon that during Beagle's angry outburst, he revealed Roy's drug involvement. His interest perked up when I told him Roy had approached me about keeping contraband hidden in the warehouse for a twice monthly cash payment and that someone would have our backs and would warn us of an impending shakedown, large or small.

Mark was convinced that for anyone to know in advance about a large institutional shakedown involving outside units meant that this was somebody on the inside of the inner loop of need-to-know, or with an unusually strong connection to that someone. If there were indeed someone high in the prison chain of command it was, yes, important, but also dangerous, very dangerous.

Mark Thurmon was not the kind of person who showed anxiety in any way, but this time I picked up on it in the tone of his voice. He reiterated the danger factor. "Jeff, back when we had our initial meeting in the commissioner's office, we were told of a confidential concern of brutality they had about someone and wanted us to look into it. A top deputy to the commissioner is a half-brother of Hayes Harvey—the subject of the complaint about brutality. If that deputy gets simple information on something like shakedowns, and might be sharing that information with Harvey, does he also get info about you? And does he share the information with Harvey?" Oh boy. Now that raised the hair on the back of my heck.

Mark tried to reassure me that no one but the commissioner and his most senior adviser, a guy named Owens, knew anything about this operation, but just to be on the safe side he would double-check and let me know what he learned. "Any doubts, and we'll pull the plug on this."

I wasn't ready to quit, and I let Mark know I'd wait to see what developed. He didn't have to remind me to watch my back and to trust no one. I knew he was a phone call away if something seemed out of place or I had a bad feeling. But I learned a phone call is not much help. Not only did I put myself in danger, but my wife, too. No, a phone call is not much help.

CHAPTER TWENTY-TWO

The following morning began with the usual pat-down of each of the guys as they came in. When I headed toward my office I felt the presence of someone right behind me. That's not a good feeling in prison. I turned around quickly to find the big inmate Matterson following me. He gave me a big smile and a nod toward the office. He had something for me.

I went to the office, and as I got to my desk and sat down he said to me very quietly, "Officer Wiles, there is going to be a delivery of goods for the inmate store this morning. We're going to lay down the rubber mats so they don't destroy our shiny concrete floors with the wheels of the carts."

I thanked him for letting me know and asked him what time. He had more to tell me than the time.

"In about an hour. By the way, if you just happen to stop the second cart and look into the top boxes you may find something of interest. If you do find something in the box it was placed there by inmate Cass Wood, who is a holder for Lieutenant Potter. The store lady who works with Potter passes it out to the inmates when they come to the store window to pick up their orders. That lady will have in her possession powdered cocaine. She keeps it in the bag she carries with the order forms."

I love news falling in my lap. Just goes to show how working with the warehouse detail pays off big. I took a moment to think of the best way to proceed with this. I decided I would make the stop appear to be a routine random search and look into several of the boxes, so no one would suspect someone informed on them.

I was on the phone with Thurmon when the caravan of store carts arrived at the back chain link gate. They let me know by banging on the gate that they didn't like to be kept waiting. Hah! They're going to be here longer than they imagined. If I find the drugs on the cart, Thurmon advised me to grab the bag with the anticipated cocaine from the store lady, Francine O'Keefe.

I let O'Keefe and her two inmate store orderlies into the warehouse. One inmate pushed a long delivery cart and the other carried several brown paper bags. O'Keefe didn't say thank you or hello. I didn't know her very well, but I had heard she'd been at RQSP for years and was an unpleasant woman to deal with. Occasionally I had heard her scream at inmates over confusion with orders, as the store is only about twenty feet from my office.

The inmate store is a 12' by 12' storage room lined with shelves stocked with goods. Inmates use order forms with prices listed to order goods. All items are approved for sale by the GDC and range from packaged ready-to-eat food items, candies, soft drinks, vitamins, hard goods such as radios, wrist watches, and ear phones. Each building is assigned a store day and time and is notified by phone and radio announcement to send inmates to the store window to pick up the items they purchased. They hand in their order forms through the prison mail system. All items are paid for in advance by money deducted from the inmates' store account, money that's been deposited by family or friends.

When the detail came through I stopped abruptly by the long cart. I looked slowly at inmate Cass Wood who was a man about my overall size and twenty years my junior; he looked to be in very good shape. Great. How much of a fight was this was going to be if I found something?

I told inmate Wood to take several steps back. Immediately O'Keefe was two inches from my face. "What do you think you're doing? We never get stopped, that really is very insulting, and I'm going to have a word with the DWS Tomley about you." She looked as if she good breathe fire.

Like that scared me. My response was quick and to the point. I looked right into her grey eyes and said, "Back away from my face, Ms. O'Keefe, and you can talk to anyone you'd like after I'm done here." I turned to Wood, who looked concerned, and I repeated my instruction for him to back away several steps. He did as he was told. I looked at O'Keefe and opened the small box and looked inside and saw several boxes of different candies and potato chips that I moved around and checked to see if they had been tampered with; they had not.

Ms. O'Keefe said in a really nasty fashion, "Happy now, let's go, Wood."

"Hold on, "I said," you are not going anywhere until I'm done, so just stay there and be cool, Ms. O'Keefe." I then moved in front of the biggest box and ripped the packing tape from the top flaps and pushed each one of the flaps slowly back, opening the top of the box for me to easily put in my hands and go through it. I did it very slowly, intentionally to make Ms. O'Keefe sweat with anger and anxiety of what I might find. On the very top layer of the contents were rows of Oreo cookie boxes. I picked each one up to examine it and noticed there were boxes that appeared to be tampered with. I opened the tampered boxes and saw small clear plastic packets instead of my favorite cookies. I pulled out the plastic packets one at a time, laid them on the side and immediately looked at the two inmates and Ms. O'Keefe. I asked her what she thought these little goody bags held, and of course she looked at the two inmates and said in a high screechy voice, "That ain't mine, it must belong to those two." I immediately took out my handcuffs and cuffed inmate David Stillwater, an older man who'd been down a long time and knew the story of how to act.

I then got my second pair and told inmate Cass Wood to turn and cuff up. He gave me an, "Ah fuck, I ain't going for this shit." Before he could resist, I grabbed his right arm at the wrist with my right hand and took my left forearm and forcibly hit him hard at the upper back of his right bicep and then pulled back and twisted his arm and he went straight down to the ground for me. I cuffed him quickly.

I turned my attention to the nasty Ms. O'Keefe. I was close enough to her to be able to reach over and take the bag with the inmate orders coming out over the top, but instead I asked her politely if I could look in her bag as well. I didn't wait for her answer. I took the bag and slowly took out all the papers, and there at the bottom of the black cloth bag was a rather nice-sized change purse of the same color and fabric. As I started to take the purse out, the sinister Ms. O'Keefe tried to yank it from my hands and yelled that it was her personal item. I agreed with her that it was her personal item, and I still took strict possession of the change purse. (I shouldn't say this, but I was enjoying myself.) I unzipped the change purse and, lo and behold, inside was the expected powdered cocaine in numerous little evenly measured packets. Bingo!

I called on the radio for the shift supervisor, Lieutenant Jackson, who responded quickly with several CERT members. They took the inmates to lockdown and patted me on the back with words of thanks for a job well done. I knew that when O'Keefe attempted to leave the prison later this day she would be met by several law enforcement officials from the GDC, Gwinnett County

Sheriff's office, and the Gwinnett DA's office.

Mark Thurmon would be the lead investigator to speak with O'Keefe, and she would be made to understand that she might not be going home for a long time depending on how cooperative, or not, she was answering questions—about who supplied the drugs she had and who else was involved.

At the end of this type of hectic but productive day, Mark Thurmon and I always tried to get together in person, but at least speak on the phone to review all that had taken place. This session was by phone, as Thurmon had been called to an urgent and important meeting in the commissioner's office and would be going there as soon as he finished interviewing O'Keefe.

I later learned from Mark that his interview with Francine O'Keefe went very well for us. He convinced her that, while her career with GDC may be at an end, she could avoid further criminal action, which would result in many unpleasant years in prison, by providing us information about those involved and how the scheme worked. Thurmon was persuasive; Francine O'Keefe talked.

You might have picked up on how disgusted I am when people aren't prosecuted for their crimes, but I knew how critical it was to get information that might save time and effort on behalf of our investigation. And O'Keefe gave us plenty of information. She told Thurmon she had been working for two years with Lt. Camille

Potter and that when it started it was just the two of them and they only dealt with small amounts of pot. Later they brought in powdered coke, crack, and small amounts of heroine. The biggest drug for them had been crystal meth. More came to light during Thurmon's interview with O'Keefe. About six months earlier O'Keefe and Potter had to start paying someone higher up in the command structure for protection from the very thing I did to them; that is why O'Keefe was so shocked that it happened to her. When I took the other two down, she thought she'd be safe—that it would only go bad for the inmates.

Unfortunately, O'Keefe didn't know who got paid or how; that was taken care of by Potter. She did know they paid a flat amount of $100 each time they brought in contraband, no matter the quantity. Potter brought it in, but if she was unable for any reason, her backup was Officer Maggy Minton.

Minton was an important find for us; she was at the gatherings Ford told me took place at Warden Barton's place. Now someone else involved in the sexual harassment investigation had come to light and this knowledge would allow us to use our new information as a wedge to get a possible statement and move forward more quickly.

Francine O'Keefe explained how she and Potter worked their game. The contraband arrived in small, easy-to-carry amounts; they brought it in on their person hidden in very private places. Now, depending on the quantity and what the drugs were, this could take place over several days or even a week. Once it was all inside the prison, they handed it over to inmate Cass Wood, who then took possession and brought what they needed on the days they sold it. How they could trust an inmate is beyond me.

When O'Keefe called for the inmates to come get their orders, she slipped them the contraband. Most of the inmates who "ordered" contraband got a quantity big enough for them to break down and sell to others. Generally, one guy from a building got the contraband and carried it back to his building in the netted store bags. Once inside he broke it down and distributed it.

O'Keefe told Mark that lately they have had occasions when inmates had their contraband paid for by someone on the outside. The implication here is enormously important. This means money is being transferred, for the purpose of purchasing contraband, from one bank account to another bank account, and never coming inside. Now I know why very little cash is ever found during large and small institutional shakedowns: there are warnings from corrupt staff and money is transferred from the outside.

But why is this important? Because it definitely demonstrates that the smuggling of contraband and the corruption of staff is far more organized than first thought. This sophistication points toward the involvement of outside groups and may even mean the presence of local gang activity. This also indicates to us that the amount of money being earned is a great deal more than GDC ever thought.

To combat this type of corruption, the GDC would have to come up with more creative responses. For example, they'd need court subpoenas and warrants to obtain suspects' personal and business bank accounts. But to get those subpoenas and warrants, far more accuracy and documentation of the collection of evidence would be needed along with much better-trained investigators.

I needed cooperation from those involved. My next move would be to contact Minton and convince her it would be to her advantage to help me and not get caught up in a criminal drug investigation. I'd let her know that we knew about her involvement with Potter and O'Keefe and the smuggling of contraband; I figured that would convince her to work with us.

Mark and I discussed the best way to move forward. He would set up a meeting with Potter and tell her we were aware of her deep involvement in contraband smuggling and that we had a sworn statement from Francine O'Keefe, which would be used for possible criminal prosecution against her unless she cooperated. Mark told me the department preferred her resignation versus her prosecution. You know my thoughts on that preference, but I had no say in the matter.

CHAPTER TWENTY-THREE

Several days later I went to see Mr. Tomley, the deputy warden of security, with the name and location of the inmate involved with laundry/barber shop Officer Rashika Crane. I had identified the inmate as Cedric Worhl of "K" building. Tomley asked if I'd be interested to help bring this to a rapid conclusion. My answer, of course, was yes.

We had the unsigned love letter to an unidentified inmate, but we did not have written proof in the form of a signed name, or a name identifying the inmate. Tomley suggested that we confront them with the letter when they were together in the laundry at an incriminating time.

With a scheme in mind to catch them together in the laundry, Tomley and I sat together in my warehouse and waited until after the inmate laundry detail had been dismissed and sent back to their buildings. I kept looking through a crack in the heavy steel front door, hoping to be able to see when Worhl left his building and headed back to the laundry to meet Crane. Just as I was about to close the heavy front door and go back to my desk to call "K" building and request that Worhl return to the laundry/barbershop to finish his work, I saw him leave his building sally port gate and head to the chain link gate of the "JK" compound. "He's on his way," I told Tomley.

The plan was to wait a few minutes before we'd walk into the laundry/barbershop. I looked out through the crack of the door and double-checked to make sure Worhl was still walking this way; in fact, he seemed to pick up the pace.

Tomley and I waited about seven minutes and then walked the short distance from the supply warehouse to the laundry/barbershop front steel gate. The steel gate was usually always locked, but must have been left open by Crane to allow Worhl to enter. But just in case, Tomley had brought with him a special security key if we needed it. As soon as we went inside the gate, three other officers from second shift followed behind us.

We entered and walked quickly into the laundry area and saw Worhl pulling his pants up fast and Crane trying to stand up rapidly from a kneeling position in front of Worhl. She almost toppled over and grabbed onto a dryer door. I went straight for Worhl and didn't have to say a word; he put his hands behind his back and turned and faced the wall.

Tomley looked at Officer Rashika Crane with outrage in his eyes, but said calmly and deliberately, "I think you are going to want to speak with me up on the hill in my office and not here in front of these fine officers and embarrass yourself any more than you have already."

Tomley looked over at me and the other officers who

now had inmate Cedric Worhl in hand for the short walk to "C" building and lockdown. "Thank you," he said, "for doing your job even when it is distasteful." The officers looked away from Crane, shook their heads, and walked out as fast as they could.

Crane was crying heavily when I saw her walking up the hill toward administration and Tomley's office. But I later learned from Tomley that Crane never showed up at his office and never officially resigned. And never officially was fired. Inmate Cedric Worhl was another matter. The department has a policy of transferring inmates who are thought to have had dealings with staff, so based on the strength of our witness statements and incident reports, Worhl was transferred to another institution as far south of RQSP as possible the very next day.

I finished the time-consuming paper work associated with locking down Worhl. When I walked out of the security office, I saw Lt. Robert Greene outside of the ID office next door. ID is the hub for split-shift officer activity and the location of the shift supervisor. This is where all incoming and outgoing inmates must pass through. It is here they will be strip-searched and have their personal property inventoried and thoroughly searched by officers before they enter or leave the institution for any reason. ID has two large holding cells that accommodate about ten inmates and is used for those newly arrived until permanent cells are arranged.

If inmates are outgoing and waiting for transportation, they would be in a holding cell as well.

Lt. Greene looked as if he were trying to avoid someone or something. As I approached, his pleasant smile appeared. With my own smile, I asked jokingly if he was out getting fresh air, or trying to avoid Officer Gilbert and her tantrums. Officer Mandy Gilbert is a good officer in charge of keeping the count of the prison correct, no easy task. She is responsible for assigning inmates to their respective cells. It might not sound very difficult, but believe me when I say it is the most time-consuming and demanding job in the prison. The assignment of inmates to a cell involves many people from the counselors to the warden, and everyone in-between. It's the type of job that sounds good, but turns out to be the most stressful, thankless position. Few can do it for very long; however, Officer Gilbert has been doing it well for several years.

Greene asked if I would I like to take a gander at the inmate in holding cell number one. I asked if we had a celebrity. He looked at me with his wide, white-toothed smile and shook his head. "Nope. Not that. Go on in and take a look and let me know what you think of him."

I bit. I admit I was curious. I opened the steel door and entered ID.

I immediately knew that something wasn't right by the awful odor that hit me in the face. I could have turned around and left, but my curiosity got the better of me. I headed for holding cell one and saw something I'll never forget.

An obviously mentally ill inmate sat on the steel bench laughing and yelling something I couldn't understand. He wore a soiled diaper and sat in his own excrement, which he had smeared all over the walls. The odor was overwhelming; no wonder Greene stood outside. Before I turned to leave, the inmate pulled two large roll-on deodorant bottles from his rectum. I had no idea what crime he had committed, but it was obvious this man needed help. When I left I told Greene that I certainly could have lived out my days without seeing that.

This mentally disturbed inmate is just the type of person who is preyed upon by inmates that I mentioned earlier who feign mental illness to get transferred to "G" building.

CHAPTER TWENTY-FOUR

Inmate Wilbur Strange is one of those people who took full advantage of the system, got transferred to "G" building, and abused less able inmates, or tried to con staff— officer or civilian. During one of his cons, he and an officer mixed it up; both lost the fight.

Officer Cyril Toms is a lean and powerfully built man in his early forties and almost six feet tall. He had spent fifteen years in active and reserve military service and had been with GDC for nine years. From the time he was in his early teens, through his years in the military, he was a lightweight boxer who had won many fights as a Golden Gloves amateur and fought as a pro boxer for several years.

Toms had taken the required classes to work in the mental health designated buildings, including "G" building. One particular day he was assigned to side two of "G" building as the range officer. At some point just after the radio announcement for first session to begin, Toms made a verbal command to the inmates on side two who were going out for first session to report to him. Like any good range officer, Toms was attempting to get those guys with appointments and job assignments out on time.

Inmate Wilbur Strange had decided that even though he had no out-of-building appointments or assignments,

he would attempt to go out anyway and wander around.
He approached Toms and asked him for a pass to the
library/school to return some books. Officer Toms did
his due diligence and contacted the school officer to ask
if inmate Strange could come over to return books.

The answer: Strange had no books out, so his request
was denied. Strange didn't take it very well; he started
yelling at Toms that he was going to go out anyway.

Toms had learned to be understanding with mental
health inmates and to give them the benefit of the doubt
whenever possible. Inmates hadn't taken any mental health
classes, so Strange kept on yelling, then he started walking
toward the big steel door that opened onto the sally port
of "G" building. Toms allowed Strange to keep on walking;
he knew that without the control room officer buzzing
open the steel door, it would remain shut. When Strange
reached the steel door and found it shut tight, he starting
screaming for the control room officer to open the door.

In Toms' defense, he tried to calm Strange and said
he would be glad to talk about what was bothering him,
but he'd have to be quiet first.

"I don't give a fuckin shit what you say, or do, Toms;
I wanna get the fuck out of here now!" Strange was in
Toms' face and suddenly swung a tight fist at Toms and
hit him hard on the side of his head. Pro-boxer Toms had
been hit like that many times during boxing matches,
or even street fights, so it was not anything that stunned
him enough to keep him from responding.

Toms punched Strange with short powerful left and right jabs just above his eyes. He hit him so many times and so fast that Strange couldn't recover enough to strike back. Within a few seconds a large gash above Strange's eye was opened and the blood poured out.

The control room officer had radioed a 10-78, the ten code used to signal other officers that a fellow officer was in need of help, fast. In this particular situation it was not really true, it wasn't the officer who needed help, but an inmate. But Strange was lucky the call was made.

When I ran through the gate of "HG" compound and saw that many officers congregated around the bleeding Strange, I knew I wasn't needed. The medical cart arrived with a nurse with a medical emergency bag and treated the bloody inmate at once. A few moments later the bandaged and handcuffed inmate was put on the medical cart for the short ride up to the infirmary. There he would be thoroughly examined by the doctor on duty and treated as required, and if needed he would have been sent to an outside hospital for further treatment. In Strange's case, he didn't require anything more than few stitches above the eye. He was then put in lockdown for attacking a peace officer. But that wasn't the end of the story with Officer Toms.

Several weeks later Toms was assigned to the main compound walkway patrol to control inmates from aimlessly wandering around causing trouble. Some of the problems these guys would cause were assaults on other inmates, robbing crews, running contraband from place to place without challenge. Warden Barton had done very little to control the problem. But by this time RQSP had a new warden; Mr. Joseph Lash was now in charge and things would change.

Toms' assignment was a newly created post, and it meant that without any exception he had to stand on the concrete walkway and challenge any and all inmates to produce passes to show they were allowed to be out of their buildings. This was a new challenge to the inmates; in the past they had been able to walk around the compound unmolested by officers and could stay out of the buildings and miss the warden's daily inspection. On several occasions, Toms was placed in the position of having to lock down inmates who would either not cooperate when challenged, or would attempt to run off. The crazy thing about running off in a tightly closed environment is that you can't go anywhere.

One rainy day when I was working at my desk in the warehouse and my inmate detail were working on their jobs, I heard the all-too-familiar 10-78 called over the radio, and the location was right outside my door. I responded and ran out the door and found an inmate lying in a rain-filled puddle of water. He was bleeding heavily from his mouth, nose and ears. I checked his pulse; it was almost undetectable; his breathing was shallow. The inmate stared at the heavens and was non-responsive. I knew he wasn't a candidate for CPR, since his heart was beating and his lungs were expanding, but I did try to stop the bleeding. I was relieved when the medical cart pulled up with two nurses to take over.

By the time I got on my feet, several other officers arrived, including supervisors and civilian staff who had been getting ready for the warden's daily inspection tour.

I looked over and saw Officer Cyril Toms standing out of the rain under the protection of an overhang with several other officers and Mr. Major, the civilian unit "A" manager. Major was talking to Toms and I figured he was getting information from his standpoint as to what took place.

Here's the story that I learned from several informants of mine: Inmate Jamie Colby had confronted Toms about something he said as the inmate was walking past him. According to my sources, who were nearby, they could hear the inmate cursing Toms. None of them could hear if Toms said anything. My informants said Colby threw the first punch, hitting Toms in the mouth. Toms took over and let fly rapid and powerful punches to Colby's face; in a split second, the inmate was down on the ground, fight over.

The end of this story comes with the end of Officer Toms. He was terminated for using more force than required to halt inmate Colby's attack, resulting in great bodily injury. I'm certain his fight in "G" building, in which he might have gone overboard, played into GDC's decision.

First, I want to say I don't condone Toms' brutality, but this kind of thing has happened before and will happen again. It is very difficult, when attacked by a predator, to know when to stop responding in kind and still maintain control of the incident. Future events will indicate that who an officer knows in high places will exact a far different result than what befell Toms.

CHAPTER TWENTY-FIVE

I was in the warehouse one early morning before the official count cleared, and my inmate detail hadn't yet arrived when I heard a knock on the steel front door. I went to open it when I heard talk on the other side. I stopped and listened and recognized Lieutenant Roy's voice; the other was a male's, but I didn't know whose. I heard him say something to the effect of "Get this done; we really need this place as soon as possible." I heard an "okay" from Roy, then two more raps on the door.

I pulled the door open in a hurry. Roy stood directly in front of me, but I still got a look at the guy hurrying up the walk. He was over six feet, had a large muscular frame, and wore the gold bars of a lieutenant on his shoulders. Lt. Hayes Harvey. No doubt.

The only interaction I had ever had with Harvey was a simple hello when we passed each other on the walkways. I had a feeling I would now have a bit more interaction than that simple hello. I now knew he was involved with the contraband smuggling, but I didn't know how deeply involved. And I sure didn't know who the big guys were.

The first thing Roy said to me was, "Okay, Wiles, you may have a 50 percent victory on this. How about if I meet you halfway? You let me put some things in the warehouse just once, and if it works out for you, maybe you'd want to do it again." She had a confident smile on her face, like how could anyone pass up a deal like that? She continued: "I'll then give you what you want. How is that for a compromise?" She looked as if she expected to see me jump for joy.

"You're talking about something important here, Roy. Frankly, I can't and won't make a decision without mulling it over for a time. "Tell you what, suppose I get back to you within the next day or so." A day or two would give Thurmon and me time to hash over whether I should join the party to set up the big takedown, of if we could do it some other way.

I rubbed a hand over my face as if I had a big dilemma. In a worried tone I said, "I really gotta think of all that could happen and how it would affect my whole damn life. I've got so much invested in working here and to put it all on the line might be a mistake." That came out like a whine. Then pensively, I said, "That's on one hand, but to ignore making some much needed cash could also be a mistake."

Roy sounded understanding. "I know, Wiles. I went through something like that myself. In fact, most other folks who are in this, or have been in the past, echoed your concerns. You're smart to think about it."
Roy just confirmed that "others" were involved, but I knew that already. I wanted to find out what role Harvey

played in this with Roy, so I went to my "go-to" guy, inmate Billy Beagle, Roy's ex-orderly. I soon found out that the charming Lieutenant Roy had made amends with inmate Beagle, and he was now reassigned to lower units as her orderly. He owed me and knew I could make his life a living hell if he did not cooperate and give me what I needed. Believe me, I had no qualms about that.

Lo and behold, who showed up at the warehouse but Billy Beagle. Roy sent him over to pick up bedding for her inmates. I got down to business and asked him how often he'd seen Lieutenant Roy talking with Lieutenant Harvey.

He'd seen them together a lot, he said, in the lower units and in the general population. "It looked like they got something going on there, and I don't mean business," he added. He didn't know what they talked about because they usually moved away, but one time he heard my name mentioned, but he couldn't pick up what they said about me. I imagined it was how to get me into their ring.

As soon as Beagle was out the door, Jose Garcia appeared. Garcia was great about getting things done for me; he seemed to be able to tap into what was happening with the inmate population that always remained hidden from most officers. Things like which inmates were part of robbing crews, and whom they were holding up, and what they got. He knew what guys were on top, and which ones were on the way out, and how they were being put out. He knew all the main inmate players and what and for whom they were playing.

The guy resembled someone that central casting in Hollywood hired when a Mexican bandit was needed. He had thick gray hair and a thicker gray mustache that curled around and down the sides of his mouth. With that and his dark complexion he'd have made a great companion, or bad guy, for the 1950s TV character, *The Cisco Kid.*

Garcia looked anxious; he fidgeted, moved around in front of the door, and when he stood still, jerked his left leg. Once in my office, he blurted out his news: he got word that the hit we had learned of awhile ago was going down in the next day or so. I asked him who the target was. He didn't know, but what he did know was that the word was coming from staff inside the institution as payback for stealing and selling out to another group.

I asked what he meant by "selling out" to another group. His reply truly bothered me. He told me there are two main groups bringing in dope and cell phones, one is staff and the other is an organized street gang.

"Garcia, you're telling me that a street gang is bringing in drugs and cells. Are they Hispanic?"

Why did I jump to Hispanic? Because a major key to the proper use of snitches is knowing enough about what they tell you to strike half truths from full reality. I knew Garcia had very strong connections to the Hispanic gangs inside the chain gang, I also knew that MS13 had been trying hard to be top dog. So his next statement didn't surprise me.

"MS13," he said. This is one of the most murderous, violent gangs now in the USA. Garcia was sure it was MS13, because they tried to recruit him a couple of years ago with money and plenty of goodies. He passed on working with them, he said, because he was getting too old to keep returning to prison, and he needed to stay straight and get out and stay out this time.

I wanted the names of the staff involved in the smuggling. He gave me those we had already taken down plus one civilian, a maintenance supervisor, Arthur Kent. He said Kent hid the drugs and cell phones in the building that houses the back-up generators. Kent's inmate detail would sell the drugs and phones and he would hide the sold stuff on the detail's tool and parts carts. When the inmate maintenance details went out onto the compound with their carts to fix things in the buildings, they distributed their orders. Garcia said Kent carried a lot of cash on his person. He knew this because he had worked on the maintenance detail in the past, and had seen it many times.

"Was the hit put out by the staff, or by MS13?"

Garcia didn't know. "All I know is it's coming soon."

This had been a very productive day. Mark and I met for coffee after work and compared notes and talked about our next move. I filled him in on what I learned regarding Roy and Hayes Harvey that would affect the direction and timing of our investigation. Mark agreed that it sounded like Harvey was certainly involved. But as of yet, we had no proof that he was connected to the drug smuggling.

Mark had news for me about the phone I had found buried under weeds. He had checked who was in the security office at the time the call was placed from there to the inmate's cell phone. There were three officers in the office at the time: Lieutenants Tuskey and Harvey and Sergeant Manes. When I heard that, I knew for sure Harvey was our guy, the guy who leaked information about the impending shakedowns. Now I had to prove his direct connection to the drug smuggling.

Mark did not want me to agree to allow contraband to be stored in the warehouse. "Sounds like entrapment," he said.

I disagreed, but learned by experience to trust his judgment. What we did agree on was to let Roy know I thought that Harvey was involved.

Our next subject to cover was the information from inmate Garcia about the hit coming soon and the MS13 involvement. I also gave Mark the news about the crooked maintenance supervisor, Arthur Kent.

There wasn't much we could do about the threatened hit without knowing the name of the target. However, we could do something about Arthur Kent. My assignment was to try to find out when something might be in Kent's possession, so we could arrange his takedown.

CHAPTER TWENTY-SIX

I told Mark I had to get away; I needed a break. My wife, Margie, and I planned a few days away on Jekyll Island. I'd be back on the job within a week.

We left Atlanta with Partouffe, our dog, and arrived on Jekyll Island after a beautiful five-and-a-half-hour drive. "Beautiful" here has two meanings. The scenery is indeed beautiful, but five-and-a-half hours and four days from prison with my wife did much to restore my equilibrium. And we hadn't even arrived at our rented condo.

We took Partouffe for a walk along the pathways and onto the beach and discussed where to go for dinner. We decided on a nearby seafood restaurant. We settled our pup in the condo and headed out to the car. I turned the key in the ignition on my one-year-old VW Passat, and BOOM!

We jumped out of the car. I grabbed Margie and we got away fast before a bigger explosion. We hunkered down behind a huge live oak—and waited. Silence. Nothing else happened.

Was this an attempt to kill me, or was this a warning to scare me? Holding my shaking wife, I can say they succeeded. I was scared shitless.

I called Mark Thurmon. He couldn't answer that question, but he did get things moving. He sent a department mechanic to check out the car. The fellow told me a sealed battery exploded, but he wasn't sure why. They seldom do that, if they ever did. He couldn't find any conclusive evidence that the car had been tampered with. He did say a very highly charged impulse hit the battery causing the explosion, but he couldn't find any remnant of an external package.

We stayed on at Jekyll Island for our four-day vacation and tried to put the incident behind us. But I learned later that was impossible.

CHAPTER TWENTY-SEVEN

I was back at work a day and getting ready to call the inmate detail to work when the office phone rang. It was Mark Thurmon and he sounded serious. " Jeff, the commissioner wants to bring the investigations to an end. And soon. He's afraid we've unraveled a hornet's nest and does not want this to continue at our expense; he's worried about the both of us. He's got a boatload of information now and knows the corruption goes deep and is highly organized. We're very close to taking down a major staff player at RQSP."

I sat back in my chair and could not respond at first. I felt like someone had hit me in the chest with a baseball bat. I could hear Mark on the other end rustling some papers on his desk while waiting for me to say something.

"True," I said, "we've been at this a long time and got a lot of information. But it's endless. We keep finding contraband smuggling networks of staff and inmate cooperatives, and as soon as we take one down, there's another one right behind it. It's more organized than just some greedy CO selling a cell phone to inmates for a couple bucks.

"Money changing hands from one bank account to

another bank account—this is deep," I continued. "My guess is the commissioner thinks the GDC needs the assistance of more experienced law enforcement agencies, people who've dealt with organized gangs and banks."

"Good attitude, Jeff. But me? I feel like he's pulling the rug out from under us. But we're not finished. He said we should finish the things we've already started and see where they lead, but not to start any new investigations if, and that is a really big if, we can. So for now we keep right on with it and see how these things shake out."

I had known that we were coming to the end. These kinds of investigations mature and never can go on forever. But we still had several things going. The maintenance supervisor, Arthur Kent, had a lot of meth to deliver on Friday. And we knew he had hidden some in the generator building. Mark and I decided we would again enlist the assistance of the trustworthy Lieutenant Greene to make the bust when Kent made his deliveries.

We ended our call and I started my day in the warehouse with the routine pat-downs. First one in to my office was Jose Garcia with affirmation that Arthur Kent did indeed have drugs currently hidden in the e-generator building. How did he know? One of his pals hid the meth for Kent, and he wanted to know if Garcia needed any drugs for the weekend. As soon as Garcia left the office, I called Mark and told him it was a go.

Two other inmates came to my office with

information. Next was Matterson who rarely got certain kinds of information, but when he did get it, it was always accurate and dependable. He told me something important was going down the next day and the likely spot would be "J" building. He could not tell me why it would be this particular building, or who was the target, but that he was almost certain it was "J" building. I paid him for his information with a pass to the kitchen for an extra meal.

My next visitor was our resident older white collar criminal, Harry Vonn. Vonn was with us for embezzling. He had almost the same information as Matterson had, but he added something that made my stomach drop.

The target of the hit was someone who was threatening to rat to investigators in turn for a transfer. I asked Vonn to give me more, but he clammed up fast and said that was all he knew about it. I gave him a pass to the kitchen and sent him on his way. I sat in my office and thought about the information from two inmates, the same information. I knew enough about prison informants to know that not all are as dependable as others, and like any rumor there may not be much to support it. But I was worried. What next?

My detail and I delivered our supplies, and as we walked back to the warehouse I heard a radio call for assistance, not a 10-78, officer in need of help. This call meant help was needed due to inmate issues.

The call came from "K" building in the same fenced

compound as "J" building. I was no more than twenty feet from the entrance gate. I told my detail to meet me in front of the warehouse. I took off running through the buzzing "JK" building gate and down to the sally port entrance. Inmate Roger Mathews was in handcuffs and being told to get on the ground by the "K" building range officer, Steven Bennet. Bennet asked me to go to cell 12 on side one and check the inmate who was on the ground. The control room officer buzzed me in and I ran down the steps to cell 12 on the lower range; the door was locked and had to be buzzed open. Oh, brother.

Between the steel bunk and the cinder block walls lay inmate Oswald Oliver. His eyes were wide open staring blankly at the ceiling with a face so purple it was almost black. He had no pulse and felt very cold. And very dead. I radioed the control room to make a PA announcement for all inmates currently inside the building to go immediately to their respective cells. Control would then lock the doors. The control room officer knew not to allow entrance to anyone but officers and to put in a call for the shift supervisor.

I looked again at the body lying on the cold concrete floor and saw what appeared to be a long string wrapped so tightly around Oliver's neck it broke the skin. Blood had oozed from the wound. I didn't touch anything at the scene, but made notes for myself and Thurmon.

I had a strong feeling about the motive of Oliver's murder. A kite had made its way to Thurmon's offices in an unopened and well-sealed envelope. The writer said he had important information and would give it up if a transfer could be arranged like the one inmate Toban got. How did Oliver learn about Toban's cooperation? But more important now, who suspected Oliver of willing to cooperate—of willing to become the latest snitch?

How did we reach the conclusion that Oswald Oliver sent the kite? It was signed with the prison nickname of double O. Many inmates in prison have all sorts of nicknames, like Paco, steel head, moocher, Jew baby. We weren't sure if the signature was double O, or if it was double zero. Thurmon solved that puzzle going through files. On the outside of Oswald's file was a notation that he was often referred to as double O. Unfortunately, Thurmon didn't catch this until the afternoon before his murder; we hadn't had time to react.

The image of Oswald Oliver lying on that concrete floor with his face turned purple from a string around his neck will remain with me for the rest of my life. I'm not sure we ever could have prevented Oswald Oliver's murder, but what I do think is that with enough time and resources we could have proven that the accused murderer, inmate Roger Mathews, was nothing more than a willing fall guy.

My investigation of Oliver's murder revolved around two inmate snitches. Both told me that inmates Roger Mathews and Oswald Oliver were very tight. Inmate Wendell House told me he knew for certain that Oliver and Mathews were more than just cellmates; they had been life mates since meeting two years earlier at RQSP. If that were so, why would Mathews kill his lover, Oliver? Easy answer: he didn't.

House's story was that Mathew's father had died recently, and his mother had to borrow money against their home to bury him. She was sick and couldn't work, so couldn't pay back the loan; hence, she was soon going to lose the house. The prevailing thought by several inmates was that Roger Mathews would not harm Oswald Oliver whatsoever, but he would take the fall, so his mother would be taken care of. Mathews was serving a life sentence for murder and because of the severity of his previous crime, would most likely spend the rest of his life in prison. He had little to lose by taking the fall. As long as he kept quiet, his mother would be financially cared for. And since he knew who did commit the crime, if the money flow stopped, he could talk. But inmate House had more to say, and I didn't like it.

Word was going around the general population that I was not a regular officer and might be involved with the Oswald Oliver investigation to find the people responsible for killing him. I, of course, denied any involvement beyond being a regular CO doing his job the best he could.

CHAPTER TWENTY-EIGHT

That very night I was at home watching TV when
I got a call from Mark Thurmon. He said he had
spoken with Lieutenant Greene about the maintenance
supervisor Kent and what he had hidden in the
e-generator building. Greene had already been told by
one of his snitches, some time ago, that someone in
maintenance was dirty and that he sold cell phones and
chargers, but this was the first he had heard about drugs.
Greene wanted to know how much stock Mark placed in
this information; without disclosing his source, he told
him it was a certainty.

Greene assured Mark he would know when Kent entered
the e-generator building because the entrance was opposite
the back gate and John Penny, the back gate officer on
duty, was a stickler about keeping tabs on all comings and
goings near his post. Greene would instruct Officer Penny
to call him by land-line or radio as soon as Kent made an
appearance and entered the e-generator building.

But what took place the next day with Lieutenant
Greene and Kent concerned me for a long time. What
followed is another example of incompetent behavior,
not the fault of the officer, but because proper training
was not offered. I was of no help; I couldn't reveal my

involvement to anyone, even to Lieutenant Greene, and Thurmon was tied up in a meeting in Atlanta with the GBI investigation of Oswald Oliver's murder. Little did I know that Mark's meeting with the GBI would lead him to soon leave GDC.

There was a flurry of radio activity involving Lieutenant Greene and Officer John Penny at the back gate. Penny needed assistance. Greene responded via radio communication which sounded like 10-4 (acknowledged request), 76 (hurrying), your 20 (location). Penny then waited for the few minutes it would take for Greene to jog from his location near the chow hall through the warehouse building. I could then open the two sets of chain link gates and one steel back door to help speed Greene to the back gate.

Once Greene arrived at the back gate, Penny joined him, as well as the kitchen officer Brownleigh. The three of them waited for Arthur Kent and his inmate detail to emerge from the e-generator building to be searched and dealt with. As the solid steel door opened and the inmate detail and Kent came out into the sunlight they were surprised to be met by Lieutenant Greene and the two other officers.

Greene searched the inmates and their tool cart and found a considerable amount of meth and two cell phones. Arthur Kent tried to distance himself by blaming the inmates; they threw the blame back into Kent's lap. Greene asked Kent if he would submit to a search, but he refused. Greene informed him that as an employee of the GDC he had to surrender to this request while still on GDC property.

Next thing I learned was Greene arrested Kent for attempting to assault a peace officer and prevent him from doing his lawful duty. The inmates were immediately locked down in "C" building. But a big mistake was made.

Arthur Kent was taken to ID and put in a holding cell with a camera on him while the Gwinnett County Sheriff's Department was summoned to pick up the arrested offender. However, it is unlawful to imprison anyone who has not been convicted at trial before a sitting judge in a court of law. The holding cell inside of a state prison can only be used to confine an already convicted felon and not someone who has just been arrested before a trial. When the Gwinnett County deputy arrived at RQSP to take Kent into custody, he knew an error had been made and informed Greene of the mistake. He said he would transport Kent to the jail, but then more than likely he would have to release him. This was a very serious error on Greene's part, so serious that it led to his demotion from lieutenant to sergeant. He would later go on to great success with another law enforcement agency.

We won something here and lost something. We lost Greene, but we got rid of a smuggler of drugs and cell phone contraband. Herein lies a major complaint of mine: lack of training. It was not the fault of Lieutenant Greene that he had never had the proper training as to how and when to make an arrest so that it would be legal and sustainable in a court of law. The reason that almost all corrections officers, regardless of rank or position, are not provided this proper training when it comes to their lawful powers of arrest is the fear of abuse and liability on the part of GDC. To prevent abuse, GDC has chosen to ignore and deny the instruction of the law that would give the power of arrest to all Georgia peace officers, which includes corrections officers. If the department would take the time to train its cadets, starting at the academy and then at mandatory in-service classes, this would assure that what took place involving Greene and civilian GDC employee Arthur Kent could have been avoided. Instead of an embarrassing incident, it would have resulted in a strong criminal case against Kent.

The Greene/Kent case wasn't the first of this type of fiasco. Over the years there have been numerous incidents in which ignorant and untrained corrections officers, who thought they could use their powers of arrest, did so unlawfully, causing untold harm.

CHAPTER TWENTY-NINE

Things were coming to a head in other investigations. Mark Thurmon and I now knew the name of the person in the RQSP security office responsible for making that early morning warning call to an inmate's illegal cell phone announcing a shakedown. It was the same person paid by Lieutenant Potter and inmate store civilian employee Francine O'Keefe for cover. It was this person who arranged the protection for the selling of drugs and cell phones through the store window. This very same person, who along with the likes of ex-Lieutenant Patt and soon to be ex-Lieutenant Roy, was smuggling drugs into the prison and hiding the contraband in places like the kitchen warehouse. The very same person who tried to make a deal with me to hide drugs in the warehouse. The very same person who caused the removal of two longtime female civilian employees.

I now believe this same person was responsible in some way for the murder of inmate Oswald Oliver. My belief is based on the information linking Oswald to a cell phone that allowed him to receive warning calls of impending shakedowns in the "J," "K," "H," and " G" buildings. The one thing that I was not able to get was if this person was being paid by inmates for his cooperation, or if he provided his assistance to them in an effort to protect his own interests—or if it was a combination of both.

There were other developments as well. One morning, while delivering supplies to the back gate with my inmate detail, I heard a call over the radio that an officer needed assistance at the Annex. This is just outside the back gate and houses inmates with short nonviolent sentences. These are the guys assigned to outside details to work on roadsides and courthouses and other locations with contracts with the state.

Penny opened the gate so I could get to the Annex to help. I gained entrance by pushing a button on an intercom attached to a steel post adjacent to the 20-foot chain link fence. This fence, as I mentioned, has barbed-wire on top and bottom, and runs the entire circumference of the Annex compound. Officer Coyote stood just outside the center control room and pointed me to an office and ran in with me. Lt. Hayes Harvey, the officer I had seen with Roy when she asked me to hide contraband in the warehouse, stood several feet back from a bloody inmate sprawled out on the carpeted office floor staring at the ceiling. Harvey told us to see to the inmate. He wasn't dead, but looked close to it. Blood flowed from inmate Calvin Meade's eyes, mouth, and ears. He had several long cuts along his face and neck. Meade had a good pulse and was breathing without difficulty.

"I'm done with the son of a bitch. I gave him his chance at me and he shouldn't have taken it." Was that his justification for beating an inmate? "Take that fool as soon as he can stand to medical and then have his ass locked down, I'll call up to security and take care of everything else."

Harvey stalked out like a powerful lion and left us with his mess. Officer Coyote and I hoisted Meade's 6'1," 220 pounds to his feet and began the slow walk up the hill to the medical department. He answered me with grunts when I asked him what caused the fight.

We dropped off our patient; Coyote went his way, and I went mine to pick up my detail. I had time to think before I got my guys and I thought back to the first meeting Thurmon and I had with the commissioner. We were asked to take a close look at Lt. Hayes Harvey due to complaints about his brutality toward inmates.

This incident happened after many, many months of accumulating evidence linking Harvey with contraband smuggling and sales, information leaking to inmates, bribery, murder, and possible links to outside gangs. Now we could add what looked like brutality toward an inmate. One problem: the inmate wouldn't cooperate. Believe me, I tried to get his cooperation. This could be the final nail in the coffin of the dying career of Lt. Hayes Harvey. But I was wrong. Very wrong.
The next morning I walked down to the disciplinary lockdown "C" building to try again to get Meade to tell

me what took place between him and Lieutenant Harvey. When I arrived I got the proverbial punch in the gut. Inmate Calvin Meade was dead. The word put out: he hung himself. I had a queasy feeling. I knew better.

He was found by Officer Marni Miller two hours earlier when she made her rounds gathering up food trays. The body hadn't been moved; IA investigators were on their way. I asked Miller what she saw; she was very willing to speak.

She had opened the pass-through flap to get his food tray and saw him in a sitting position against the back wall. A rope around his neck was tied to the steel bars in front of the tiny open window. She opened the cell door, called for assistance, and went in to see if he was still alive. His face was purple; he had no pulse and was cold to the touch.

I asked her if anyone else had been in the building. She couldn't swear that no one else had come in, as her partner, Officer Dobbs, was busy on side two breaking up a fight, and she was tied up checking twenty-five solitary cells on side one.

Whether or not anyone saw Harvey, this is the second time in a matter of weeks that an inmate death is related to him. Suicide? It's not easy to strangle oneself with a rope around the neck when it is tied to steel bars in front of a window that is no more than four feet off the ground. And that's how Calvin Meade was found. There would have been no downward angle in which to create leverage sufficient enough to strangle oneself, as is supposed to have happened with Meade. No matter, I guess. The death of inmate Calvin Meade was determined to be suicide by hanging and the case was closed. I will never be able to accept that conclusion. I spoke with the investigator who arrived at that conclusion. He told me he had no experience with suicides or murders in prisons. Another example of ineptness in the Georgia prison system.

CHAPTER THIRTY

Mark and I agreed that we had enough circumstantial evidence over a long period of time to take the name of Lt. Hayes Harvey to the commissioner. We discussed the timing of when we should do this. Right away, or wait until Mark had his scheduled interview with Lieutenant Roy. We decided to move forward before another horrific incident occurred.

I learned to rely on Mark to get back to me within minutes after a meeting with the commissioner so I would know how to move forward, or even if I should move forward. He didn't let me down and called my office landline. But as soon as I heard his voice, I knew I wasn't going to like what he was about to say.

"I know you're fucking going to strangle me when I tell you Harvey has been transferred from RQSP effective this morning to some damn Transitional Center in south Georgia."

Mark was only half right; I didn't want to strangle him, but I did want to kill the someone responsible for that transfer. I said through clenched teeth: "Someone in that freaking office is running interference for this guy. Who is it?"

Mark took a very short second to respond. "A deputy

commissioner and he happens to be related to Harvey."
Before I could spit out an invective, Mark continued.
"Want to hear what I found out asking around about the
bullshit politics?"

I knew I'd be even more depressed but I listened.

"Okay, we now know about the deputy commissioner,
but listen to this. In 2000, Harvey was fired by the
department when he was a CO for forcing one male
inmate to demonstrate a blow job on another male
inmate. A complaint was filed and investigated. The
outcome of the investigation led to his termination;
however, one year later he was reinstated. So far that's
all I got, because his early personnel file is nowhere to be
found. But I put my money on the deputy commissioner
as the turd who made reinstatement happen."

But Harvey wasn't just reinstated. He would be
eventually promoted to the important post of deputy
warden of security and returned to RQSP in his new
capacity. He later left RQSP when he was promoted as
warden at another high-security state prison. While he
was warden there, several inmate murders occurred.
Numerous high-ranking uniformed supervisors were
later quoted in news articles that Hayes Harvey's policies
were to blame for the murders. In addition, they said
he leaked information to inmates warning them of
impending institutional shakedowns. Exactly what Mark
Thurmon and I had uncovered years earlier, Harvey
carried with him to another prison. I'm grinding my

teeth here. Harvey and those like him should have been prosecuted.

What Mark said next would really change things.

"I'm leaving GDC. Soon. I'm going with the GBI."

My mouth fell open. Mark went on, "I feel bad, real bad about leaving you high and dry like this. We made a great team and you've done an incredible job. The commissioner knows that without you doing what you do by putting yourself out there we could never have gone as far as we did." Mark wasn't finished. "Uh, he's leaving too."

Oh, man. I felt as if my life raft had just sprung a leak.

"Don't worry, though," Mark said. "Before he leaves he's going to make sure you move onto something else and out of harm's way."

Mark said he had planned to wait until after the Harvey business was disposed of, but that was now a done deal. He wanted a chance to interview Roy and see where that would lead us. He said he'd leave when I thought the time was right. As it urned out, Roy left on her own and didn't wait around to be fired or arrested. Do you see a pattern here? Not many arrests at GDC, just a lot of "retirements."

Over the next two weeks Thurmon and I finished paperwork and said our good-byes to each other. I'll always be thankful that I had the chance to work with a guy who had such integrity about his work and commitment to do what was right. And he always had my back.

A short time later Commissioner Jacobs moved

on. Before he left, though, he did prove he was a man of his word. I was promoted to the position of transport sergeant effective immediately and would spend very little time working in the prison. I guess he thought I'd be out of harm's way. I know I did. But it wasn't to be.

I was in my new position for two months when the noise awakened me. When I knew gunshots had been fired. When my wife jumped out of bed and I flew across it and pushed her to the floor. When I stood in the street and looked at my neighbor's house pockmarked with bullets. Bullets meant for me.

I didn't wait for an investigation of the shooting. I'm out of the prison business for good.

EPILOGUE

The relationship between officer and inmate is a very complicated one that can often be misunderstood by anyone not familiar with prison culture. This culture is many thousands of years old and has been handed down from generation to generation with very little change, even though the outside world has indeed changed significantly.

Survival of the fittest is the most powerful ingredient in this culture and it affects all those who must deal with it on a daily basis. Officers and civilian staff who are given the critically important responsibility of working with the inmates who live in this prison culture can never be trained well enough for what will confront them once on the inside.